T0354890

THE STORY
OF THE
ROYAL BABY

OTHER RELEVANT BOOKS

The Magnificent Case of the Royal Baby
The Curious Case of the Royal Family
The Auspicious Case of the General and the Royal Family
Life is Good
A Tale of Discovery
Shelter on Place
A Case of Espionage

THE STORY OF THE ROYAL BABY

HARRY KATZAN JR.

THE STORY OF THE ROYAL BABY

Copyright © 2024 Harry Katzan Jr.

All rights reserved. No part of this book may be used or reproduced by any means, graphic, electronic, or mechanical, including photocopying, recording, taping or by any information storage retrieval system without the written permission of the author except in the case of brief quotations embodied in critical articles and reviews.

This is a work of fiction. All of the characters, names, incidents, organizations, and dialogue in this novel are either the products of the author's imagination or are used fictitiously.

iUniverse books may be ordered through booksellers or by contacting:

iUniverse
1663 Liberty Drive
Bloomington, IN 47403
www.iuniverse.com
844-349-9409

Because of the dynamic nature of the Internet, any web addresses or links contained in this book may have changed since publication and may no longer be valid. The views expressed in this work are solely those of the author and do not necessarily reflect the views of the publisher, and the publisher hereby disclaims any responsibility for them.

Any people depicted in stock imagery provided by Getty Images are models, and such images are being used for illustrative purposes only. Certain stock imagery © Getty Images.

ISBN: 978-1-6632-6390-2 (sc)
ISBN: 978-1-6632-6392-6 (hc)
ISBN: 978-1-6632-6391-9 (e)

Library of Congress Control Number: 2024912210

Print information available on the last page.

iUniverse rev. date: 06/19/2024

For Margaret Now and Forever
With Love and Affection

CONTENTS

INTRODUCTION

The Royal Monarchy of the British United Kingdom is a wonderful thing. It serves as a model for the world to behold and exemplifies how peoples can work together to achieve common goals.

The Royal Monarchy works as a team to achieve goals that would not be achievable by individuals and traditional organizations. The Kings, Queens, Dukes, Dutchesses, Princes, and Princesses work tireless hours to achieve those goals. Most members have work that require activity requiring 300 days or more in a single year.

The British love their monarchy. But, so do the people in the entire world.

This book is a short story of the Duke and Dutchess of Bordeaux and their activity to have a royal baby. It is very tedious and heartwarming.

This book is entitled *The Story of the Royal Baby*, and is an update and improvement of its predecessor to *The Mysterious Case of the Royal Baby*, published in 2019.

The author is a Professor and an author of computer books. The author claims to be an author but not a writer. You know the rest of that story.

The book is for readers of all ages. It contains the author's tradition of *no violence, no sex, and no bad language.* Please enjoy the story.

Harry Katzan, Jr.
June, 2024

PROLOGUE

Matthew Miller and Ashley Wilson met in a college creative writing course and became good friends, spending time together in the college library and at the local Starbucks coffee shop. Their academic studies were as different as they could be and their family backgrounds were also quite different.

Matt, as Matthew was normally known, was a math honors scholar with a strong interest in pursuing a PhD from a prestigious university and then becoming a math professor.

Ashley was a drama major interested in pursuing a career in drama. Both were good looking: Matt was exceedingly handsome, tall, and athletic, Ashley was extremely pretty and looked like a movie star. She had a good figure and all the rest.

Their backgrounds were also different. Matt was from an established U.S. family. They had disposable income but wouldn't be classed as wealthy, except for Matt's grandfather, who was formerly an Army General, PhD, and founder of a successful political polling company. He was wealthy and liked to help people.

Ashley's family background was totally different. Her father, who had a PhD in theatre, worked in the movie industry. He enjoyed an important position that offered little recognition. Her mother, who also had a PhD, was a dance professor at an Ivy League university. They are divorced and live separately.

Ashley's father was Caucasian and her mother was African American. Ashley classed herself as being biracial, even though she was thought to be white by others, and generally regarded as such.

The story picks up with short descriptions of the persons involved with this rare and unusual scenario, as well as the mysterious lady on the road in England.

ONE

ABOUT MATT AND ASHLEY

Matt had found himself a nice quiet spot in the reading room of the university library. Each department had its own library, but it was nice to be alone when doing math problems. His professor, straight out of Harvard, advised his students to copy their notes and do the assigned problem set as soon after class as possible. He was doing just that, when, out of the blue, Ashley appeared. "I thought I'd find you here," she said, "you look very busy."

"I was doing my math homework," Matt replied, "I usually do it right after class." "That's impressive," said Ashley, "Are you a four point oh student?"

Matt was in fact a 4.0 student but he didn't respond to the question directly, but after a few moments finally responded with, "Just doing my job. I'm in the middle of a lengthy proof, so have a seat, and we can study together."

This being exactly what Ashley had hoped for, she fumbled her way around the table and gracefully sat down.

After looking up, down, left, and finally right, Ashley said, "I think I'll take a look in the stacks."

Matt looked up and said, "It's the other way."

Ashley sheepishly replied, "It is my first time in the library. Drama majors don't usually go to the library. It's nice though."

"I should have guessed that," Matt answered, "You're very pretty and have a way with words. I'm kind of finished. Would you like to have a coffee, or something like that?"

"Sure," she said and off they went.

The two students inadvertently headed towards Starbucks, and on the way, Matt pulled out a gift card and asked, "Is Starbucks okay?"

Ashley replied, "Of course yes."

Matt said, "That's from Fiddler on the Roof, Right? For sure you're a drama major."

"Caught in the act." She said.

"The reason I wouldn't mind going to Starbucks is that I have all these Starbucks cards. I have about six of them. A couple from my parents, a couple from my grandfather, and some from athletic shoe reps. The reps take you out for a coffee ostensibly to ask you about your success with their shoes, and then say 'keep the card'. My grandfather tells about during the war, if you went out for a smoke, the greatest thing that could happen was when the other soldier just said 'keep the pack'."

"Most people don't ever refer to their grandparents." Ashley quipped. "Are you and he close?"

"Well, yes and no." answered Matt. "Sometimes we play golf and sometimes we play tennis and sometimes our families go on vacation together – especially when he and my grandmother feel like going to Hawaii. He pays for my education that includes tuition and fees, dormitory room, dining hall, books and supplies, and spending money. I think he would like me to work for his company when I graduate."

"Do you want to?" asked Ashley.

"I guess so." Matt replied. "He owns that famous company that makes opinion polls. I've worked there during the summer and the work is pretty interesting for a person interested in analytics and stuff like that. But we'll see."

They reached Starbucks. She ordered a 'grande' skim latte with two shots and he got a 'grande' coffee. They found a good seat by the window. She continued the conversation. "Are you a math major? It sounds like you might be one."

Matt continued. "Yes I am. Do I act like one?"

The response was almost automatic. "No, not at all. Actually, I thought math majors were stuffy and aloof and things like that, and you're not that way at all."

Matt chuckled. "I guess some of them are, but most of us are pretty normal. A good student has to keep up with the work, and if you don't, it's hard to make it up like you can in some reading courses. So math majors appear to study a lot"

Ashley was quick to respond. "Remember that first day of class when we had a coffee break.

Professor Purgoine said she wanted to talk to some students and you were one of them. Was that because you are a math major? It is a bit unusual. A math major taking a writing course."

Matt answered both questions. "Yes it was and it was also about my physical appearance. She looked up the records of each person in the class. She thought I looked like an athlete and found that I am on the tennis and golf teams. Another thing. She found that I am in a fraternity. She was afraid that I was some jock that took the course only to meet girls. I explained that I realize that I have taken a lot of math courses and need some variety, and that my grandfather, who is paying for all of this, advised me to take a writing course are the two reasons why I enrolled in the course. There is another aspect of the situation, which is that I enjoy the process of writing as it provides a way of creating a little world of my own. I also read pretty much fiction and have read two of her novels. I made sure to mention that."

"So it looks like it turned out pretty well." Ashley remarked. "Are you wealthy?"

Matt laughed a good belly laugh. "No, I am nothing other than a poor college student. My grandfather has made a lot of money, and my parents have decent paying jobs. My grandfather told me once out on a golf course that he always wanted to be an author, but he chose business because of the depression and all of the people that suffered. He said he didn't want to be poor, even for a minute."

Ashley was so engrossed in the story that she didn't even drink her coffee. Matt said, "You haven't touched your coffee. Let me get you a warm one."

Thanks to the miracle of gift cards, Matt returned in minutes with a two-shot skim latte that Ashley accepted graciously.

Matt continued with a quick remark, "to continue, my mom teaches third grade, my dad works for the company that makes and scores SAT tests, and I have one brother and two sisters. Now, how about you, my dear friend."

Ashley hesitated briefly somewhat overwhelmed by the apparent simplicity of Matt's life and his complete openness about his personal life. "Well," she started, "my family has done well, considering, but my life is more complicated than yours. My parents are divorced. My mother teaches dance at Yale and my father makes movies in the LA area. Actually, he doesn't act in the films, but puts the filmstrips together to make the film. I think it's called postproduction but maybe that's not exactly the real name of what he does. My mother is a total pain; she's always calling my professors to make sure I get a good grade, and she's always bugging me about studying and boys and just about everything. I have a brother and a sister who have graduated from college, but I don't know exactly what and how they are doing. My father is a bit like your grandfather; he wants me to do well but mostly he wants me to be happy. He's also a bit like you, I think, because he doesn't worry about things, and cheerfully takes what life has to offer."

Matt smiled. "Thanks, I will take that as a complement. Let's finish up. I have to go to golf practice. The coach was the NCAA wrestling champion, and now he is the golf coach. Imagine that. He doesn't even play golf, but he yells a lot and is consistently on our case. I might know more than he does - about golf - but that is a story for another day. We practice at the country club and take a university van. I really don't want to be late. Would you like to run into each other again?"

"Sure, sure would."

"I propose we meet at the same time next Tuesday in the library. Would that be okay with you," Matt asked.

"It's fine with me."

The two students hit the street with feelings of time well spent.

TWO

ON TO THE GENERAL

As mentioned in the prologue, the main characters in this story are the General, Matt, and Ashley. Other people pop up here and there, but they are the most important people. Here is a snapshot of exactly who we are talking about when we refer to the General in the ensuing chapters.

Les Miller, the grandfather of Matt, is a retired three star general officer who achieved a rank of Lieutenant General in the U.S. Army. In civilian life he is referred to as *The General*, because of his record of accomplishment in and out of the military. He holds bachelors, masters, and doctorate degrees and is the founder of a prestigious political polling company. The following snapshot also includes Lt. Charles (Buzz) Bunday, the General's wing man, and the Air Force commander during World War II. In the following paragraph, the eventual General is Lt. Les Miller.

The following scene begins the General's scenario. The Air Force commander and Buzz Bunday are waiting for Lt. Les Miller to return from his bombing mission in the new

U.S. fighter plane known as the P-51. As the saying goes, if you have a P-51 on your tail, you're a goner – that is, the enemy. The fighters normally accompany and protect bombers, such as the B-17 that are on a bombing mission against the enemy. In this instance, Miller is on the tail of a German fighter plane that shot down a U.S. B-17 bomber. Buzz radioed Miller to forget the enemy because he, Les Miller, might use up his fuel. Tired of waiting for Miller to return, the flight commander said, "He's either run out of fuel or been shot down." Buzz, who is Miller's buddy, replied, "Let's give him a few more minutes." The commander answered, "You've got 2 minutes Lieutenant. I've got work to do."

"I hear something," said Buzz. "It sounds like a 51. It's him." The commander replied, "His engine just shut off, must be he's out of fuel." Les Miller, the General, makes a dead stick landing and runs into a barrier, put up for that purpose. The General jumps out of his P-51 and says, "I got him, he's a goner. That is 36 kills for me." The commander turns and says that the two lieutenants should report to him in the morning at 8:00. The two pilots have completed the Air Force requirement of 25 missions and are quite proud of themselves, as most fighter pilots are shot down before they make the minimum requirement. All Miller says is, "That is why he is a commander; that man has no feeling about other people."

In the commander's office at 8:00 the next morning, the pilots enter and salute the commander. "At ease gentlemen," says the commander. "By my records, you have completed your Air Force requirement of 25 flights. Attention! You are now promoted to the rank of Captain, U.S. Army Air Force, with all rights and privileges pertaining thereto. In your case Bunday, you have the British equivalent. Both of you have two weeks leave in the states and are then ordered to report to the Pentagon for duty or assignment. Your expenses are covered by the government. Good luck." That was the end of World War II combat for the General and Buzz.

The two pilots enjoyed their two weeks in New York City, along with a fine hotel and good food. Buzz, born and raised in England, is amazed by the quality of life in what many Englanders refer to as the colonies. As World War II servicemen, the men appreciate the famous Statue of Liberty given to the U.S. by France. They agree that it is quite impressive.

At the Pentagon, Captain Miller and Captain Bunday were ordered to report to a high level secret meeting concerning the number of P-51s shot down in a single mission, which is roughly 60%. The command of the U.S. and Britain believe that a failure rate that high cannot be sustained in terms of personnel and equipment.

The Air Force tried titanium panels as armament and the method did not work. So, the big guns were brought in to solve the problem. The meeting is being attended by three-star generals, college professors, and noted scientists. They laugh when the Captains are introduced. "What good are a couple of Captains when the smartest men in the country cannot solve the problem." The problem is well defined. All of the bullet holes are covered up but the planes continue to be shot down. Captain Les Miller says, "I can solve the problem." The others just laughed and they took a coffee break. Buzz says, "Les, are you out of your mind? You're probably going to get us demoted."

Les replied, "Don't worry Buzz, I'll solve the problem."

"What did you major in in college?" asked Buzz.

"Math," said Captain Miller, "but as I said, don't worry about it."

"I certainly hope you are right," said Buzz.

When the meeting got going again, Captain Miller was asked to describe the method that he says will solve the problem. Here is Miller's response. "The objective of the meeting is to determine where titanium plates are to be placed for protection of P-51s. Here are some photos." The photos showed P-51s with bullet holes. "The planes have been plated where the holes are with no improvement. Now, that is the reason why we are here. It's an easy problem." The rest of the audience just laughed and looked at each other. One officer mentioned so everyone could hear him. "This guy is a joker. I thought that was why they were here, to help us solve the problem. The new Captain is off his rocker."

Captain Miller calmly continued, "It's easy gentlemen. The important holes went down with the plane – in fact, probably caused it. Look at the photos, do you see any planes with holes in the bellies, for example. We should plating areas where there is no holes."

The audience just looked at each other."

"If the Army Air Force armor would armor plate the untouched areas evident in the photos we have, the problem will be solved," said Miller.

The armor plating was placed in clean aircraft bellies, and the percent of shot down planes was reduced to 10%. Note, this is a true story. Captain Miller, and his buddy Bunday were promoted forthwith to the rank of Major. Again, this is a true story. The author has researched it and read the descriptive math paper that describes it. A distinguished professor worked on it for some time.

There is one more description of the General and how he eventually and implicitly inherited the title of General. As is commonly the case, an Army officer must obtain a promotion within a certain time period. If there is no open slot, then he or she must retire as an officer. That is the Army way. It happened to General Les Miller, even though he had several remarkable episodes, such as landing a transport plane, filled with officers and also generals, when the pilot and co-pilot were disabled, and he received an another field promotion.

General Miller was forced to retire as a three-star when no promotion was available. The number of generals is governed by the congress. Once out of the service, the General called his friend Bill Donovan from the Nuremburg war trials. Donovan defended Gary Powers in the famous World War II trial and eventually became President of a university in Brooklyn New York. Donovan said to General Miller, "I was once in your position Les, why don't you come to my university and get an M.S. in computer Science? We have one of the finest masters programs in the world, if not the first, on the subject." The General did just that, getting his MS degree and meeting some Iranian students, one of which is portrayed in other episodes.

The General used the knowledge he obtained from his MS degree in Computer Science to build a large political polling company. He gained an enormous fortune and gained the reputation as a person who used his wealth to help people.

The General eventually received his PhD in International Relations, as an officer in the Army, where the time and money for his studies was granted for outstanding personal achievement. That is the Army way.

The General was and is an avid golfer, being a member of a local country club, at which he and his grandson Dr. Matt Miller played at least twice in a week. The General also established an upscale restaurant named the *Green Room*, that he used for business and pleasure.

The General owns a personal aircraft named the Gulfstream 650 that was purchased with personal money. A few years later, he obtained a small business jet for short trips. The General was an experienced military pilot having flown P-51s, B-29s., and the B-52. He never piloted his own personal aircraft.

The General's first wife died early on and he eventually married Dr. Marguerite Purgoine, a professor at a local prestigious university, and known by the moniker Anna, who was Matt and Ashley's writing instructor.

The General has numerous friends in the Army. One of which is General Mark Clark, four-star Chief of Staff, and eventually Director of Intelligence. The General is also the friend of the President and the First Lady.

THREE

THEN THE ENGLISH LADY

One more thing concerning the general. After the P-51 problem was resolved, Major Les Miller's new job was straightforward. All it amounted to was to check returning P-51 flights and perform an assessment of damage from interactions with the enemy. Again, this was during World War II. Then, based on relevant analytics, initiate protective measures. Aircraft vendors would be there to assist him and actually perform the necessary updates. Then, go to the next air base and do the same thing. The plan was more than obvious. After changes are completed, he would certify deployment and analyze returning flights to insure the protective measures were working. The travel between bases in England was treacherous and often involved travel over muddy roads. When a trip was lengthy, it necessitated sleeping in a pup tent and eating K rations. Actually, the K rations weren't that bad and the kit usually contained a chocolate bar and a pack of Lucky Strike cigarettes. The officers also had nylon stockings to give to the local residents.

The relationship between U.S. servicemen and English country folk was usually quite pleasant.

Miller's master sergeant was a likeable fellow, and he and Miller got along splendidly. The sergeant was nicknamed 'Bud', and he was a big muscular guy – an ex-MP. Along one long stretch of muddy road, they came upon a young woman who had slipped off the road while driving a light military truck. Actually, Miller, driven by Bud, passed by her for security reasons and then returned to offer assistance. It turned out that she was a Second Subattern (i.e., a second lieutenant) in the women's Auxiliary Territorial Service. Her specialty was mechanics and truck driving. Assisting with the war effort was an honorable thing to do for women at that time in history.

"Are you okay?" asked Miller.

"I'm okay," she answered. "I'm just a bit frightened. I've been off the road for a long while and thought that no one would show up to assist me. You are Americans?"

"We are both Americans," answered Miller. "Let us help you."

The jeep, a remarkable little vehicle, pulled her out of the mud, and the conversation continued.

"We are traveling to RAF Grangemouth air base," continued Miller. "We work on airplanes."

"You are a Colonel. Do you fly airplanes?" The pretty young woman asked. "My name is Mary Wales, by the way."

"I am a pilot," answered Miller. "My name is Les Miller and my driver is Sergeant Bud Small. By the way, would you like some chocolate, or cigarettes or nylons? We have chocolate and cigarettes from our K rations, and they give us nylons to give to women that we encounter. We know that some items are not available in England."

"I would appreciate some chocolate and nylons. I'm very hungry and have been waiting here – off the road for a long time."

"Are you sure you don't want cigarettes?" asked Bud.

"No thank you, I don't smoke," said Mary. "Smoking is bad for you."

"That's probably true," said Bud. "Some people don't care. We don't smoke either. That's why we have them to give away."

"You are very brave," said Miller. "Most women don't want to help out with the war effort. You look like my sister. She is very beautiful."

"Thanks for the complement," replied Mary. "Can I give you a good old British hug?" Miller replied, "Sure, and I'll give you an American hug in return."

After the hugs, Mary replied, "That is the first hug I have ever been given. People don't touch me."

The remark was left unanswered and the two vehicles went on their way in opposite directions.

"Nice looking girl," said Miller. "I hope she makes it wherever she's going."

"You bet," answered Bud.

The updates to P-51s turned out to be successful and the loss rate went from 60% to 10%. The European war was over in a few months, and for the most part, the hostilities ended, even though there were a few skirmishes from time to time by axis fighter planes.

FOUR

ABOUT THE PLAY AND GOLF LESSONS

The week passed quickly, as Ashley and Matt were busy with normal student activities. They exchanged pleasantries in the writing course but otherwise didn't see anything of each other. Ashley accepted a promising part in a university play and was extremely busy learning the script and becoming accustomed to working with the other cast members. Matt was typically occupied with pleasing his golf coach and a load of mathematics homework. Math majors usually work toward a Bachelor of Science degree with fixed requirements in the traditional sciences and mathematics. When you're a math major, your mathematics courses are your major subject and also satisfy the requirements for graduation, yielding additional free electives. But since most math majors love their subject matter, it is customary for them to take additional mathematics courses as electives, resulting in more problem sets to work on. Ashley spent most evenings rehearsing and Matt spent most evening doing problems. They were both anxious to see one another.

Matt got to the library first as his last class was in an adjacent building. Ashley arrived a little later with a sheepish grin on her face. She remarked as she walked to the table. "I hoped you would be here. Did you miss me?"

"I was looking forward to seeing you." replied Matt. "How was your week?"

Ashley answered in turn, "Oh I have to tell you, I got the best part in our new play. I'm so lucky. We will rehearse almost every night. Actually, we just got started and haven't accomplished that much except getting to know each other. I have read the entire script."

"Congratulations. I'm sure it wasn't luck. You had to be the best person for the part." said Matt.

"I have to tell you a big secret. A real big secret."

"Well you better tell me all about it before you burst." said Matt.

"Have you heard of that British play named 'Mousetrap'? It's the play we will be working on, and the one we will present to the audience."

"I've heard of it. It's supposed to have been running since the 1950s or something like that with a surprise ending."

"When the play finishes, the audience is asked not to reveal the murderer," said Ashley.

"I suppose that's to keep the play going." said cool-headed Matt.

"The director told us that Agatha Christie, who wrote the murder mystery, said that she would not reveal the surprise finish in another book. But she did and the title of the secret book is Three Blind Mice and Other Stories."

"So who is the murderer – the butler?" said Matt jokingly.

"No silly, there's no butler in the play. It's the detective! The play is really great."

Finally Matt said in a serious manner, "I'm really pleased to see someone so happy about a project like you are because I'm sure it will be a lot of work to put it on."

"Oh, the director is very nice. I'm sure he won't holler at us like football coaches yell at players and call them dumb, like I've heard." Ashley replied immediately. "But, you never know. He might if the actors foul up with their parts." Ashley continued, "So, how about your week?"

"I do have something I wanted to tell you, but it is not as spectacular as your news. But first, would you like to have a coffee? I have a new Starbucks card. Now I have eleven of them," said Matt.

Ashley replied in the affirmative and they headed off to the local Starbucks.

On the way, Matt mentioned that his golf had improved considerably and that he had won a college tournament over the previous weekend. The golfers only played two rounds of 18 holes, but it was still called a tournament even though it was a small competition for local universities. In fact, he had done so well that the coach talked to him of going pro after graduation. Matt indicated that he wasn't pleased with the idea, because he had thought that teaching or doing analytics would be something he would like to do to help make a difference in the world, and was not so sure about running all over the country playing golf and having a hectic social life.

They got to Starbucks and both ordered a caramel macchiato. Ashley was surprised.

She said, "You've changed. I thought you were a stuffy old mathematician, and here you are ordering a special coffee."

"The shoe rep talked me into it. It was quite good, so I wanted to see if the second one would be as good as the first. Right off, there is something I want to explain to you. Remember last week when I said I might know more about golf than the coach. I guess it sounded like I have this big ego. There is more to that story. Much more. First, I'm not the kind of guy to make derogatory statements about someone, like a coach or a professor. In this case, there is something that happened to me a while ago."

"Is this very serious or personal? If so, I don't want to hear about it." Ashley asked.

Matt responded. "Oh no. It's not that kind of thing. First thing, my grandfather wants to be squeaky-clean and is very particular about appearances. He has a prosperous business and makes an enormous amount of profit. He never uses the business for his personal use. All the money he spends on family and personal things comes out of his bank account. Second, he bought himself a big airplane and likes to use it. He was a pilot in the war and has the license to fly an airplane, but has a professional pilot to fly this big one. Let me back up for a minute. I started playing golf when I was young and played pretty much. I was a good player and had the physical attributes to play even better. Now, all of this happened between my high school years and college.

I was fortunate enough to get golf lessons from the pro at the local golf course. Actually, it was a country club. Then my grandfather invited a European pro golfer and his wife along with their daughter to the US to give me golf lessons. He provided the golfer and family with a luxury car for a vacation after the lessons. He paid the pro golfer a fortune and even sent his plane to Europe to pick them up and fly them back."

"How long were those golf lessons?" asked Ashley.

"They were almost a month and we covered really advanced topics like spin and slicing in a useful manner and how to get out of hazards and all kinds of things. This was after I had already received advanced lessons from the local professional. When he got finished with me, I was young, energetic, and a strong amateur golfer. I think I had been given everything I needed to be a really good player. All I needed was a lot of practice."

"That is really something," said Ashley. I know you are a good person, but why did he do all of that?"

"I don't really know why he does all he does, but it seems to me that he just wants to do the right thing for people and his family, but doesn't want to waste his money. Maybe, some of the things he does for others are things he wished he had when he was young. He does that with business and political donations and just about everything."

"Does your grandmother go along with all of this?" asked Ashley.

"I think that she not only goes along with them but encourages him."

'I think you're rich and are acting like a poor student."
Ashley injected with a sly grin on her face."

'I guarantee you that I'm not. All I have in my personal
bank account is a few hundred dollars in spending money. If
I wanted to do something like go to Florida for spring break,
I don't think I would have enough to do that." answered
Matt.

"Okay, let's say you wanted to do something really special,
could you ask your parents for the money?" asked Ashley.

"Yes I could – ask them, that is. They would ask me
what I wanted to do, and if they thought it was worthwhile,
they would give me the money. But I wouldn't ask. I'm just
happy that I have the opportunity to go to a good college.
I like being a student. It's very possible that I actually am a
stuffy math major."

"You don't seem stuffy to me, but you are serious. Don't
you worry about the future or what you're going to do in the
future?" asked Ashley.

Matt replied without thinking, "Nope. I just want to be
the best I can in whatever I do and try not to be concerned
with what options the world has for me. But, you haven't
mentioned anything about yourself. Are you happy? Are
you rich? Do you have big plans for your future in whatever
you plan on doing? You dress extremely well and look like
a movie star. I think you are a cut above the rest of the girls
around here."

Ashley was pleased to respond. "Thanks for the generous
compliment. I do want to be somebody, like a well-known
performer or a princess or a person that's known for something
other than helping to raise a bunch of bratty kids. I want to

be someone that I want to be and not someone that the world thinks is good to be. Does that make any sense at all?"

"It does to me. Isn't that free will? We are all free to choose what we want to be, as long as it is something that's reasonable. Not everyone can be President of the country or the CEO of a multi-billion dollar company or a major-league baseball player. Maybe it all depends on what kind of things you like to do. There are steps leading up to a goal and if you don't like the steps, then you probably aren't going to reach the goal. Sometimes you want a job that another person has and is good at it so it's not available to you. Sometimes a person is qualified but is in the wrong place at the right time," added Matt.

Ashley looked puzzled and said, "That's what bothers me, and that's exactly what I think about. There may be something in the way so that I can't get there, whatever there is. No matter what a person does, the goal might not be attainable."

"You have to choose the right goal at the right time, and you have to be the right person for whatever it is. You might be a great basketball player, but you are not going to make the team if you are five feet six inches tall." said Matt sympathetically.

"Well, I guess this is a subject for another time." Ashley replied. "As far as being rich is concerned, I am not either. My father pays for my college and my mother pays for the social things, such as clothes, entertainment, and travel. So I'm not exactly poor. My father is extremely valuable to the film company he works for, because without his knowledge and experience, there wouldn't be any movies. I suppose he has a very good salary. He has a PhD in something from the UCLA film school, but hardly anyone knows about it. The president of the studio knew about it when my father was hired 30 years ago but he, the president, has since passed away and hardly anyone knows about my father's education. My father says that is how he likes it. My mother also has a PhD; it is in dance and her life is a complete mystery to me. I was almost totally raised by my grandmother."

'I have a solution for you." Matt said. "Marry the prince of a kingdom, like Monaco. Grace Kelly did it. You look as beautiful as she did."

"Yeah right. What am I supposed to do, go over to Monaco and say, 'Hey prince, do you need a wife? I'm available. I was in a school play once.'"

"I have to go to practice. Let's get out of here."

FIVE

GRANDFATHER AND THE MASTERS

The time passed quickly and Ashley and Matt saw very little of each other outside of normal class meetings. Matt was exceedingly complimentary of Ashley's work when classroom discussions involved the writings of the course participants. Professor Purgoine was excessively pleased with Matt's work and frequently expressed literary amazement over the manner in which he formed disjoint concepts into a harmonious whole. At one point, there was a lengthy discussion over whether mathematical theory was an acceptable means of expressing literary concepts. Most persons thought it was simply the case that the teacher liked the student.

As is normally the case, the mid-term assignment of a moderately short story snuck up on the students in the class, and the usual complaints ensued. When the professor checked on the actual progress of the class, only a few students had even started to work on it. True to form, Matt, who was used to doing his homework regularly, was only a couple of days from turning in his final copy. Matt was popular in the class so his work ethic was readily accepted. Professor Purgoine asked to look at his work and the agreeable Matt acquiesced without hesitation. As she leafed through the pages, her only remark was "This is really good work." And then continued with, "Are you sure you are majoring in the right subject?"

As the class ended, Professor Purgoine asked Matt if he would consider reading his paper aloud. Always quick to please, Matt responded with, "I can read it but don't you think my voice is a bit too dull for a classroom presentation?"

"No, you will do just fine."

"Okay then I'll do it," said Matt..

Ashley and Matt left the classroom together. As they struggled down the three flights of stairs, Matt asked Ashley if she would like to have a quick lunch at Starbucks.

"Do you have a new Starbuck's card?" asked Ashley.

"Nope. Just have something to celebrate. It's not really that great. My mother called with some news, and I thought that maybe it is important enough to celebrate a little. Also, some other things have come up of a personal nature. Anyway, how can a person celebrate around this place? All there are around here are students, faculty, and who knows what."

"You have fraternity brothers and you have me," said Ashley.

"That's why I asked you. Deal or no deal?"

"Of course yes. How can I refuse? You're pleasant, optimistic, and never complain." Ashley replied.

"You are the best. Thanks for the compliment. I think you are going to wind up being rich and famous, and I will be going around saying, 'I know Ashley Wilson'."

Both chose a Starbucks sandwich, a bag of chips, and some iced coffee. Ashley wanted to sit in a quiet corner and Matt agreed in his usual manner, "Okay with me." It seemed as though everything was okay with Matt – at least to Ashley.

Matt initiated the conversation, "I guess you are wondering what the big celebration is." Remember, I said it was nothing great.

"Well, what is it?"

"I got my pilot's license. It came in the mail. I have an instrument rating so I can fly in bad weather. Now you're going to laugh. My grandfather wanted me to be able to land a plane in case the pilots become disabled."

"Why would he want you to do that?"

"You know, I really don't know for sure, but we think it happened during the war. He was a fighter pilot but was riding in a transport plane when the pilot and co-pilot got shot. He was able to land the plane and save everyone. He got a medal for it."

"He must be famous."

"I don't know if he's famous, but he ended up being a general in the Army Air Force. He never talks about the war so I don't know much." Matt added.

"He must have connections all over the place," replied Ashley whose attention picked up.

"I sure don't know anything about that, but I have something else that bothers me a bit. The coach got me into the Master's golf tournament in Augusta as an amateur. I have this hard mathematics course and I really want to be the top student, so this disrupts things. I want to go and don't want to go. I guess I can take my notes and the textbook." I don't think I could say I don't want to go to it."

"Maybe you'll get a green sport coat."

"You have to win the tournament to get the green coat. I don't think that the green coat is for amateurs."

Ashley and Matt were quiet for a few moments. Finally, Matt opened up. "I really don't like to talk so much about myself. What about you?"

"We're still working on the play and it's not that much fun. The director gets mad and the players respond by not doing very well. Then the director gets more and more angry."

"Just like football, Matt added. "Basketball is even worse."

"This isn't fair. We do all the work and the university gets all the money. I'm tired of all this rehearsal. Who cares?"

"If you become a professional, then you get paid. That is how it works. It's a gamble, and some people think it's worth it." Matt replied.

"Do you?" asked Ashley

"Do what?" asked Matt.

"I mean to do all this work for a university on a gamble." Ashley said.

"Well in sports, some people just like to play football or basketball or whatever. I really haven't thought much about it. Sometimes I get tired of talking about money. It seems that is all people nowadays think about. At the moment, all I'm interested in is graduating."

"I'm interested in drama to become well known and then money should follow along with that. Right now I'm worried about my short story for our writing course. I don't have a great idea and I need some help getting started." Ashley was getting worked up.

"Let's meet in the library today after our last class and before practice and rehearsal. I'll go over what I did so you can get started. I don't think she wants miracles."

SIX

ALL ABOUT MATT AND ASHLEY

Ashley and Matt met at the library, as planned, and headed on to Starbucks. On the way, Matt reviewed what the professor had covered about writing a short story and emphasized the notion that a decent story needed a strong beginning and an even stronger end point. A good short story has to make a difference in the make-believe world of that episode.

When they got to Starbucks, the coffee shop has entered the dull period just before the dinner hour. Good tables were readily available. Many students eat all of their meals in fast-food establishments, even though their sponsor pays for a complete meal plan at the university. Most students have their dirty clothes washed at the washateria down by the natatorium or even send their dirty clothes home in the suitable container purchased in the campus bookstore. Of course, some students do not have any clothes washed at all and resort to buying new garments when the need arises. The subject of living on campus seems like a suitable subject for a story and Ashley quickly picks up on it. Then she asks Matt to give a rundown on his planned submission.

Actually, Ashley asks for a copy of Matt's story, but Matt refuses, which is uncharacteristic of him. Ashley doesn't seem to mind.

Matt starts the description of his short story with a rundown of the characters and then continues with the events that are pertinent to the plot. He then finishes with the end scene, which turns out to be the main point of the whole episode. There is an unusual similarity between his story and the scenario that was taking place before his very eyes. He wonders a bit about it but then continues as planned. Matt smiled as he says, "You asked for it. So here is a quick summary of my not-so-short story. Interrupt if you dare."

"The story mainly involves two students enrolled in a writing class. Both students are serious about their education. The male student is easy going with a strong interest in his major field of study. The female student was interested in fame and fortune. Both students have good financial backing and their relationship is above board and platonic. He is a good athlete and belongs to a fraternity. She is very pretty with excellent social skills and a knack for dressing well. The male student is named James Rogers and little is mentioned of his athletic ability and fraternity activities. He is devoted to his major field, which is mathematics, and spends an unusual amount of time working on his mathematics problems. The female student is named Emily Taylor and her academic interests are not described, except that she is a drama major and has a part in a play. Emily is biracial, which James has determined through her behavior, interests, and general mannerisms. Emily is surprised that James could determine her racial characteristics. Her heritage is derived through her mother, who is African-American, and her father, who is Caucasian. James is not interested in a romantic relationship at this time so the differences are not of general interest."

"Both students graduate and there is no further contact between them – at least for a while. James finishes his education and becomes a mathematics professor and serves as an analytics consultant to the family firm. Emily, on the other hand, has a storied career. She goes to New York with the hope of furthering her prospects for success. Opportunities are limited and she works at odd jobs. She marries a good prospect for success in her personal life, but it is not enough. She meets a foreign worker in a nightclub who befriends her and provides hope for the future. It is not a romantic relationship. She is fed up with her husband's old-fashioned idea that hard work will get them somewhere and divorces him forthwith. Her newfound friend named Arthur Street introduces her to a member of a royal European family. After a variety of relationships, the royal, known as Prince Joseph, and Emily fall in love and are married. The marriage is generally frowned upon by the populous because of her American background and her American way of doing things. A baby is expected from the royal couple early in their marriage, but Emily does not want to get pregnant. The racial characteristics of an expected baby might become an issue to the royal couple."

"Emily meets with Arthur and explains the expected problem that might arise in the birth of the offspring. The royal couple is afraid of having a baby with off-white skin and other characteristics that might be unpopular to the royal establishment. After a series of private discussions on the subject, Emily mentions the short story written by a college friend. Arthur explores the problem with the college friend who arranges for a surrogate mother using the sperm of the royal husband, stored for emergency in a secret sperm bank. Timing is crucial. The plan is to have Emily emulate the development of a fetus with padding that would look like a baby bump. Immediately after the surrogate baby is born, it will be transported to Europe with the fast airplane and transferred in secret to royal couple's home."

"Emily will then go into make-believe labor at that time the surrogate baby will be announced as the royal baby. The royal family and the country are fooled and life proceeds at its normally slow pace. Emily is deeply depressed over the incident and commits suicide, disguised as an after birth incident."

Matt smiles and says, "That is my story – in brief. Of course, there are other options and situations."

Ashley looked directly at Matt and asked, "Do you know that I am biracial?"

Matt answers, "Not for sure, but I thought that perhaps you were."

"How could you suspect that. I never mentioned it, and I know for sure that I don't look or act like I am African-American." answered Ashley.

"But you do. It's a cultural thing. It's the way a person approaches a situation, looks at a problem, gives an explanation of something complicated, reacts to a surprise situation, and so forth. If you add up all of those things, you have a profile of someone."

"That's not true," said Ashley.

"But it is. I can pick out a person with a strong math background, for example, in fifteen or twenty minutes. We can work together productively because we solve problems and even approach problems in the same way. I went to school with African-American students – usually the same persons – from kindergarten to the twelfth grade, and I was on sports teams with them for most of that time. In short, I have experience with persons of diverse cultures, and that is precisely how I could get some intuition on your background," said Matt.

"I still don't know about that."

"You've heard about people that can complete another person's sentences. Computer programmers do it all the time."

"Can you read my mind? Do you know what I'm thinking?"

"Of course not silly. It's not that kind of thing. It's overt behavior that anyone can see or hear or maybe even feel if they are tuned in. Actually, you're thinking that I'm a bit crazy but it's true. Football and basketball players do it all of the time, when they play together as teammates. So do coaches. So does your mother."

"Well okay. I believe you. Will you help me with my short story?"

"Sure. I will help you. But I want you to recognize that the story that I have just told you is a representation of the interaction of what is going on between you and me. In math, it is called recursion, and I think Professor Purgoine expected that."

SEVEN

GRADUATION FROM COLLEGE

The last six weeks of their final semester was complete chaos for both Ashley and Matt. The Mousetrap play was in total disarray, as the basic characters of the performers didn't exactly match the requisite characters in the play. Last minute adjustments kept the performers busy until late hours, and most students had other courses with which to contend. Matt, who had completed his creative writing assignments helped Ashley with hers, as he had agreed to do.

Matt was busy with his own work, which was an honor's work paper. The handy Starbuck's cards were an absolute lifesaver, and somehow or another, all of the academic work eventually got done.

Matt graduated with high honors and honors in mathematics and Ashley got a low honors award, but was quite pleased to have graduated. The graduation ceremony was another form of chaos. Ashley's mother had her own graduation ceremony to contend with on the same day as Ashley and Matt's, and Ashley's father had a firm deadline on a film in Hollywood. All of the Miller family attended and Matt's grandfather and grandmother treated everyone to a magnificent dinner in the university's special residence. Matt took the occasion to announce that he had been accepted in an accelerated two-year PhD program in mathematics at a renowned university, and the grandfather was proudest of them all.

Matt's family was extraordinarily cordial to Ashley, even though they hadn't seen her before. Ashley was beautiful and, as usual, dressed as a high fashion celebrity. There was a touch of reluctance by Grandfather Miller that was not detected by anyone except Matt. Working at the polling company and hours on the golf links had given Matt and his grandfather an insight into each other's emotional intelligence. Something wasn't right, although Matt couldn't exactly put his cognitive thoughts into words.

Matt gave has parent's address and phone number to Ashley as well as his cell number. Ashley couldn't reciprocate because she was headed off to New York to start a new phase of her life. She didn't relate any insights into specific plans and Matt thought it was better that way.

That evening Matt and his grandfather went out after dinner for a walk around campus. It was nice to be alone with your best buddy – using the concept rather loosely. The grandfather was unusually tense and Matt asked, "Something's bothering you. Right?"

"It's something about your friend Ashley, but I can't exactly put my finger on it. Do you have a romantic relationship with your friend?"

Matt laughed. "No. Not at all. She is only a lonely soul that I met in my creative writing course – the one you talked me into taking."

"Was my advice useful?" asked the General.

"Of course. You're always right. But I think I have detected what you have detected. You might not even know it yourself. I picked it out the first time I met her, but I can't exactly describe how I drew out what I am going to tell you. She's biracial. Half African-American. She even said so."

The grandfather smiled as he has never smiled before. "That must be it. You're a genius my boy. A real genius. Since then, have you figured out how you knew it?"

Matt said, "I'm not exactly sure. It's in the way she approached a situation, responded to uncertainly, how she solved a problem, and how she answered a simple innocent question. I've been on teams with African-American men and gone to school with them since kindergarten. It might be true of all cultures. You must have the same intuition from the military."

"I do, but it isn't that. Some people are strangely afraid of Generals. She wasn't. I have to think about it. You're probably on to something Matt. It must be all of those mathematics courses you took. You have a great life ahead of you.

"Thanks grandfather. I think I owe it all to you."

EIGHT

THE NEW ASHLEY

While Matt was reveling in his newly experienced success, his friend Ashley was experiencing the frustration of most aspiring performers. Her father wanted her to enter the expanding and lucrative field of film production and even offered to pay for an advanced degree or two at the best California University. Ashley, who could be as sweet as any individual on earth due to her drama training, thanked him profusely and refused. Ashley's mother wanted her to enter academia and offered to support her study in a relevant PhD program. Again, Ashley refused. Instead, she moved to New York, took up residence in a YWCA, and secured an agent. She even considered adopting the stage name Nicole Wilson derived from her legal name Ashley Nicole Wilson.

The agent, who gave free advice and other services to aspiring actors and actresses, advised her to go into the film industry. His standard advice was, "I've been an agent for fifty years and here I am making a modest living in the nation's most competitive business – acting. Take my advice.

Go to California. Get another degree. Then go into film production.

The rewards are numerous and the golden state is the country's most pleasant place in which to live."

Ashley replied as an experienced performer, "Mr. Roth, you are the nicest person I've ever met, and I believe you are sincere and also correct. That is, from your point of view. But I want a more prominent role in acting and New York is the only place to start."

"Well, if you really feel that way about it, all I can say is 'good luck'. I'll help you all I can." He replied.

"Then please tell me how to start." Ashley asked.

"Get a job as a waitress for the evenings and go to acting school during the day. You will, in all probability, learn nothing more than you already know – as you have graduated from one of the nation's most prestigious drama universities – but that's how you obtain your entry to the seemingly closed acting community. Just remember, there are many other young ladies floating around with the same ambitions that you have."

"Okay then," Ashley replied, "thank you for all you've done." Ashley Nicole Wilson collected her possessions and started to leave Roth's office.

"Wait. Wait. I might have something for you." Roth called her back. "I may have a new slot that just came in," said Roth.

"Is it in drama or something related?" Ashley asked.

"Not exactly, but it is a good start. It is an exceptionally good start. A lady I know owns and operates a form of upscale entertainment center named the Bon Chic that hosts parties and other festivities for large businesses and wealthy clients. Her name is Lydia and she runs a tight ship. You receive training on how to behave, how to dress, and how to execute the firm's business of hosting. They provide the uniforms and teach you precisely how to act. In the running of her business, she requires strict behavior for both clients and employees. No drunkenness is permitted and employees are restricted on how to engage with Bon Chic clients. After you finish Lydia's school, you certainly don't need acting lessons, but then again, it's not my business. Do you want to give it a try?"

"Well then, okay. I'll give it a good try. I really appreciate your help." On the way out, Ashley realized that she didn't even know the salary, but that was a minor consideration at this stage of her career. After all, she'd only been in New York for a few days.

Ashley was happy and pleased with her ability to emphasize and articulate precisely what she wanted out of life. Matt was right in thinking that if you did not like taking the steps necessary to realize a goal, then perhaps that goal is not the one for you. She thought about Monaco. It would really be nice to go up to a Prince and say, 'Hey Prince, looking for a beautiful wife? I'm available.' She would like to talk to Matt and get his opinion on the situation. Or just have a cup of Starbuck's coffee. Then she thought that Matt was too sensible for her. All he would say was go to California and get a degree in film production. I wonder how this Bon Chic is. I hope I get the job. Maybe a movie producer will come in and see me and invite me in for a screen test.

NINE

THE ENTERTAINMENT CENTER POSITION

The Bon Chic Entertainment Center was in need of suitable workers, and Lydia was exceedingly particular about her assistants, as she called the persons that worked for her. Ashley's beauty and perfect figure won Lydia's heart during the initial interview. By the following Monday, Ashley was ready to go. Ashley progressed nicely as did the Bon Chic, located in New York at 48th street and 7th avenue, previously the home of Mama Leone's restaurant noted for its bougie delicacy and generous portions. It is a prime location and the Bon Chic took advantage of it. Ashley quickly became a manager and met an associate named August Getraub, an import from Germany who Lydia thought was a perfect fit for her type of business. Also a Bon Chic manager, Getraub took a liking to Ashley and tried to advise her concerning career choices. He quickly recognized that Ashley was biracial and attempted to assume the role of mentor, which she readily appreciated.

It didn't take long for Ashley to get a bit restless in her temporary profession and accepted minor roles in various TV commercials and drama productions. Ashley even became a suitcase girl in a popular game show. While agent Roth could not do any more for Ashley, aspiring agent Getraub was a hustler who could. After a little less than two years of trying, Getraub secured a position in a TV show for Ashley. It was a major role in a production based in Canada. In only two years, Ashley had succeeded in the competitive world of drama. Finally, she was a performer who was widely known and her name was recognized in the world of show business. She had an insatiable appetite for success and nothing would step in her way and block her path.

Another thing that Ashley did to further her career in her magic two years was to undergo minor plastic surgery on her nose and lip line. Also she straightened her hair and applied skin lightener as a part of her personal makeup routine. Ashley was perfect in every way and possessed a gracious personality to go along with that exemplification of supreme excellence and the world would soon know it.

TEN

A LOOK AT SHOW BUSINESS

Playing a major role in TV production is an extremely demanding job. On day one the cast meets and the director goes over the script, scenery, and supporting activities. Productions differ. Some are a continuous series of episodes with continuity between the shows. Others are independent productions with standard performers and differing plots. Still others are plays that run the same script multiple times, and lastly, others are film stories. The cast is usually comprised of seasoned performers, so by the end of day two, everyone knows their lines and the dramatic sequence. On days three and four, the sequences are assembled, and the dress rehearsal is performed for day five.

The show is taped on day five and the production is broadcast nationwide on day six.

Some scenes are taped multiple times at the discretion of the producer, director, and writers. The production is edited in the afternoon and evening of day five and released over the distribution channel for the various time zones early on day six. The cast is off on day seven, but for the management people and the creative staff, it is a 24-7 operation. The support staff, such as costumes, scenery, make-up, and so forth, has a dynamic schedule depending upon the nature of the production. At first, a new show is mass confusion, but after a couple of weeks, things settle down to a harmonious whole.

The TV industry has adapted the concept of 'season', wherein a show runs for approximately nine months and the remaining portion of the viewing year is supported through re-runs. This fact, along with the obvious fact that performers essentially grow into roles, enables the performers to have an ample amount of free time during the production period. As one could easily imagine, Ashley used this free time to enhance her professional career and as one might readily assume, her social calendar, taken in this context, was varied and extensive. She socialized with all manner of entertainers, politicians, celebrities, and people from business.

ELEVEN

AN APPROPRIATE SOCIAL CONNECTION

Ashley liked working for Lydia at the Bon Chic. Lydia managed with strong authority, and that was totally different from the total chaos on the stage and screen. Through effective human relations, Lydia got the most out of her employees, including Ashley and August. August moved up into administration, and Ashley's role diminished for obvious reasons – she was becoming a drama star. August was always fixing Ashley up with likely suitors, and that usually worked out fine, since Ashley liked to have a good time. There was always a tension between Ashley and a strong person with a good education and that didn't usually match with her expectations in blind dates.

There is always a viewpoint when discussing social interactions. From the woman's view, most men are looking only for entertainment and shy away from any serious conversation. From the man's view, most women are looking for a husband or at least a meal ticket.

Things changed when August introduced Ashley to Prince Michael of European royalty, who was on a diplomatic visit to the United States. He was different. He liked to talk about intellectual subjects, and instead of spending an evening drinking, he preferred to spend a quiet evening in hospitable surroundings. He was interested in discussing opera, ballet, dance, and serious politics. Ashley liked that.

It was one blind date and then back to Europe for the Prince. Ashley thought that she would never see him again.

Lydia was entrepreneurial and opened a Bon Chic in London. She asked August to manage the transition, and since Ashley was in her off-season, she was asked to help August set things up. Ashley liked the idea of living on an expense account, and besides, was attracted to the glamour of the London theatrical scene. August introduced her to a whole host of well-known performers, influential business people, and an independent press agent who took a liking to the idea of furthering the career of an up-and-coming American actress. The press agent, known professionally as Pamela Givens, talked incessantly of turning Ashley into a global brand. Pamela re-united Ashley with Prince Michael and a friendship flourished.

Prince Michael was ripe for a social change, and Ashley was the one to do it. They attended tennis matches together, dined together, and spent leisure time together. They had become an item.

The tabloids were abuzz with expectation and, initially, Ashley could do no wrong. Michael was a bit of an independent sole and nearly everyone knew it, especially the royal aristocracy. Ashley changed all that. Michael became domesticated and very popular.

When their engagement was announced, the news media was on fire. Ashley's part in the TV show was cancelled as public performance was one of the taboos of the royalty. A fall wedding was planned, and the paparazzi were in high gear.

TWELVE

A GLORIOUS GRADUATION

Matt Miller awakened to a warm sunny morning, almost two years to the day of his first graduation. The two years seemed to fly by. The PhD courses were interesting. The professors were knowledgeable and enthusiastic, and he had little difficulty with the subject matter. His dissertation went smoothly. He had selected a relatively new math subject, namely Categories and Functors, so he knew the salient points of the subject that most people on his committee had no knowledge of.

As before, the Miller clan gathered to celebrate the occasion. For this celebration, they needed the Gulfstream and a professional captain and co-pilot. The grandfather was pleased, since the plane was not exactly overused. Matt's mother and father were extraordinarily proud as he had gone six years of university study and had received all As. That gave exceptional bragging rights.

After the family dinner in the university's private dining hall, Matt's mother asked him a very interesting question.

"Matt, do you know what has happened to that friend from college days? I believe you called her Ashley."

"No, not at all," replied Matt, "Did she do something important? She always wanted to be a famous performer. She was a sweet girl."

"Maybe she has. There is an actress in a serial TV show by the name of Nicole Wilson who looks like your friend."

"If she looks like my friend, it's very possible she is my friend Ashley. Her middle name might have been Nicole." said Matt. "We don't have a TV where I live. Anyway, I normally am too busy to watch TV. Did she call?"

"Someone called for you and it sounded something like her. It sounded like a female voice." Matt's mother replied. "Old people just worry about things. That's how we are."

Matt just smiled. Nothing could dampen his good spirits. "I'm sure it's nothing. She probably just wants to brag that she is a real actress, if that was she. That was always her goal. I don't think that she wants financial help. Her family has plenty of money. I do not know who it is that could have called."

"Have you decided to take that offer at the local university that you wanted so much." Grandfather Miller, the General, asked.

"I have accepted the offer, and I am very pleased to be working as an analytic consultant for your firm. I'm going to try the academic life. If I like it, get some publications, and even get tenure, then I might seriously consider it as a career. Otherwise, I'll try other options. You've forgotten that I'm still young. I'm only 24 years old. You guys talk to me like I'm an old seasoned veteran."

"You're a doctor." Matt's mother said, "That means something."

"I've been very fortunate to take extra math courses early on and was able to finish my degrees in six years, and of course, thanks to all of you ."

THIRTEEN

A PROBLEM: A BIG ONE

Back in London, August met with Pamela in a quiet no-camera restaurant. August chose wheat beer, and Pamela selected Swiss white wine. Both knew it would be a serious conversation, because of the choice of restaurant.

Pamela initiated the conversation after the usual pleasantries were offered. "I think we have a very serious problem with Ashley's biracialism, and there is no upside to this situation. You did inform me of Ashley's biracialism, and we tacitly decided it was not an eminent problem. Ashley has not exactly kept it a secret. To her, it is a non-issue."

Pamela continued after a short pause. "Things have changed with the engagement and wedding announcement. Once the media gets wind of the fact that Ashley is part African-American – one half to be exact – the Queen and the rest of the royal community will try to kill the wedding for sure."

"Maybe not," answered August.

"How can you even think that, much less, say it? The people around here don't even like each other. What would you expect when a royal descendant marries a woman that is half black. If they have a child, who knows what will come out. You must have observed the American military floating around in Europe. The man is black, the woman is white, and they are escorting a black child with fuzzy hair."

"You may be right."

"I know I'm right. And the Queen won't do a thing. The royalty is always under pressure around here. It's not America, where things just blow over in a relatively short time. It could even kill the aristocracy," Pamela was getting worked up.

"Can we work something out?" August's military training snapped into gear. "We need a plan."

"We don't even know the extent of the problem," Pamela said.

"Okay, here's what I think," replied August. "The people – now I mean the taxpayers and politicians – will stand for a biracial wife to a royal descendant to the crown, but they will not tolerate a biracial kid. Never. That's just the way it is in this country. Even in America, some of the African-American people don't like biracial people. It's my own opinion, but I think it's at least half true."

"So the problem is the kid and not the woman," replied Pamela.

"Yup, that's about it. At least that is what I think. But let me say something about the whole situation. This person that we know as Ashley is a pretty good catch. She's beautiful, intelligent, educated, experienced, and loaded with good ideas. She may appear to be a bit of a gold digger, but I suppose that's part of the situation. There are people that will not like her, no matter what. Let me have a long talk with Ashley, and I'll get back with you. Ashley likes me and I like her. She's the most level headed person I've ever met." said August.

"Even more level-headed then me?" asked Pamela.

"Don't be silly. You know I think you are the best. But I mean all the rest. On this subject, no telephone and nothing written. The media and government service have their claws into everything and everyone."

"Can we get together in two days," asked Pamela

"Let's make it three. I might not have immediate access to Ashley. The royals have a tendency to control everything and everyone's time, as well. Remember no telephone."

"I'm glad that you're in this with me August," said Pamela.

"That's the same way that I feel." replied August. "There is one more thing, that I learned in the military. You shouldn't shoot a person until you know he is the enemy. We don't really know whether or not, that Ashley is really biracial. Perhaps, she just thinks she is biracial, or someone told her that she looks biracial – although that is very unlikely. Or her mother made a derogatory comment to that effect when she was angry over something that Ashley had done."

"Maybe she just wants people in both races to like her," continued Pamela. "We probably will never know for sure."

FOURTEEN

ASHLEY RECOGNIZES THE PROBLEM

August proposed a business lunch with Ashley including Pamela at the Pub Around the Corner, the same restaurant where he met with Pamela. As one would expect, both parties were cordial. It started with friendly smiles and a big hug. The three people liked each other.

Ashley started the conversation. "Thanks for the kind invitation. Now that the wedding has been announced, the total control of me has started. It's like being in prison, every move I make is monitored and scrutinized. 'Do this and do that.' Every move I make is watched. The only place where I feel private is in the loo – that's what the royals prefer to call the bathroom – and I'm not so sure I have any privacy there. Your call sounded urgent. What's up?"

August answered very quickly. He had been anxious to say something. "You remember when Pamela and I were discussing your background and your situation, and we think there may be an upcoming problem."

"Do you mean because I am American or that I am biracial? You know me August. I try as hard as I can to be squeaky clean."

"It's the biracial aspect of your pending marriage. Remember, this isn't America." answered August.

"Michael knows and the Queen knows, and anything they know, the whole world knows. I have heard some negative things because I am American, but not a word about my biracialism. Okay, I don't hear or see everything, but I have supporters that even like me – at least I think they do."

"It's not you," said August. "It's the baby. It's a big deal around here, and as you know, there are a lot of people that do not have enough to do."

"Michael and I have discussed the baby aspect of the situation, over and over, and we haven't come up with a viable solution or even an absolute conclusion," replied Ashley. "Michael is wonderful. He thinks of everything. The whole family and the aides think of everything, and that's a real problem. They buy things for me – especially clothes. If they can't decide between two dresses, for example, they will invariably buy both. I'm sure that when we are married, the media will report that I have spent hundreds of thousands, where in reality, I personally haven't purchased a single one. I do not need money, and I am not going to marry Michael for financial reasons. I've read that some people think I am a gold digger, but I guarantee you that is the farthest thing from the truth. My mother and father are doing very well; they are not wealthy but are close to it."

August chuckled and then replied, "I don't think that is much of a problem."

"On the surface, it probably isn't," said Pamela. "Except when children are involved. Most people think it's best to keep the children out of the spotlight for as long as possible. Once the public becomes disinterested, they are not as relevant anymore and a child can mature normally."

"The public expects you to have children as soon as possible after the marriage ceremony." said August. "I have also heard, that if you don't have heirs after a certain period, you lose your royal titles."

"We realize that the public and the royalty will expect a child at the earliest time possible, and we understand their viewpoint, but we are deathly afraid that the biracial background of mine will turn out to be a huge liability." replied Ashley.

August abruptly changed the tone of the discussion. "Are you trying to tell me that you need an exit strategy from your forthcoming marriage or the baby situation in case things go bad?"

"I hadn't thought of it in that way," answered Ashley. "I feel we need a strategy, but not necessarily for exiting. Michael and I are a good team and we enjoy each other's company. We think the same. We are an item. I love him dearly and I think he feels the same, as I do.""

"If you felt it necessary to exit from the royal scene, would you do it with Michael or by yourself?" explored August.

"Michael has spent his whole life, so far that is, as a royal and I wouldn't want him to leave. I guess we need a strategy to take care of the baby situation. So it isn't actually an exit strategy, but a strategy that concerns the color of the child. I might as well tell you that we have spent hours on this subject. Michael is a big planner, so the subject is getting to be serious. He plans everything, except our current problem." Ashley answered.

"So I guess the question is, 'Do you want me to help or not?' And if the answer is yes, then do you personally want me to plan it out to your satisfaction, or let you guys plan and I do it." replied August.

"I would say both," said Ashley.

August sat back like the man who could solve any problem, waited a moment, and then asked, "What have you come up with, so far?"

"We started from the beginning. The first question was child or no child. That refers to me. If we choose no child, then we have two options: live with the problems of not having a baby and the public, or fake the birth and have a surrogate mother to carry a baby and serve as its nanny after birth. Another option is to have an unrelated nanny or not have one at all. I have a friend in college who wrote a story on this particular subject in a writing course. So I kind of used his ideas in the way I approached the problem. That is, so far. Then, what comes next? I would like to hear how you arrange the rest of the plan. We could fake a pregnancy with padding and by staying out of the limelight as much as possible. We already have a reputation for wanting to run our own lives."

"But with a surrogate mother there would be no royal blood in the baby," said August with a smile on his face.

Ashley smiled. "We're way ahead of you on that one. The royal family by statute is now required, at the most appropriate time in a subject's life, to deposit sperm and eggs, as the case may be, in a sperm or egg bank, respectively. In my friend's story, the sperm is transferred to the U.S. by appropriate means – such as a relatively fast airplane – for subsequently implanting the sperm in a surrogate mother. As the fetus matures, the fictitious mother wears a plastic pad that grows in a realistic manner. When the surrogate mother gives birth, the baby is transferred here to its intended place of birth that is probably an instance of home birthing, which is the traditional procedure in some countries. The birth is announced and the surrogate mother can be employed as a nanny, which is not necessarily necessary. The baby is officially royal, because a royal sperm was used in the surrogate's fertilization."

"It could work," replied August.

"In the second case," continued Ashley, "the royal mother – the intended mother, that is – really gets pregnant and carries the fetus to term. If the baby is white, then things are fine, except that an African-American form of DNA is passed on. I don't specifically know the scientific language for all of this, but that's the ides. Now, if the baby is black, then we live with the situation or the baby is still born and is replaced by the surrogate baby."

"I know I'm playing the devil's advocate here, but with the first option, i.e., the surrogate mother option, insures the subject of biracialism could be stopped with the royal mother by not having more kids. That would be you." said August.

"But what if the mother, that's you again, really wanted to have a child?"

"That is precisely why we haven't come to a final solution." Ashley looked tentative at this point.

"If you can stand it after all of this, let's have some lunch." said August.

Ashley agreed to the lunch and wished she had her cool-headed mathematician friend from college to consult with. Ashley wondered if that would still be possible.

"I have to go the loo," said Ashley. "I'll be right back. Choose something really scrumptious for me."

"That Ashley is really a sharp chick," said August. "She is a lot more than a pretty girl."

FIFTEEN

ASHLEY CONTACTS MATT AND SOMEONE CONTACTS THE GENERAL

The aristocracy is in a crisis. A royal wedding is always a crisis, because most of the royal staff is accustomed to doing almost nothing. It's not even imaginable how many servants are involved in the making of a slice of toast for the Queen and then delivering it and finally cleaning up afterwards.

The paparazzi also are in high gear having to have new batteries installed in their iPhones with which to take spy photos. There is nothing but the best for the darlings of the British media. All of the tires on the royal limousines need to be replaced for the three-mile journey from the palace to the church.

Prince Michael has plenty to do, having to explain all the details of the ceremony to the Queen. Surprisingly, Ashley has almost nothing to occupy her time, since she now refuses to do anything when someone is watching, which is nearly always. She wished she could talk to the calm and collected friend from her college writing course. He would know what to do. If he didn't, he would just figure it out. She googled his name and voila, she found in mere seconds that he had received his PhD and now is employed as a professor at their alma mater. True to form, the university has his full resume online including his course schedule, office phone, home phone, and email address. Also included is his private cell phone number. Bingo, she thinks, this is better than a slot machine on the Riviera.

So Ashley Wilson, soon to be Duchess of something or another decides to send her old friend a message to ask his opinion on an important subject. She expects him to be guarded but cordial, since they have not seen each other for some time. But then again, he might give some good advice. He is a brainy math professor and she is a well- known international celebrity. Ashley decides to send a message to Matt.

Initial message from Ashley:
Hi Matt, this is Ashley from the continent across the sea. Do you remember me?

Matt replies:
Hi, I was just thinking about you.

Ashley thinks
Liar. Is that what they teach in PhD program? You never lied before.

Ashley continues:
How are you doing?

Matt replies:
I'm fine, Just getting started here in my first semester.

Ashley continues:
I have a big problem and think that I might need your opinion.

Matt replies:
Just tell me about it, I'm still good at solving problems.

Ashley continues:
Here it is. I'm going to marry this royal prince, and we're expected to have babies. We are concerned that the baby might come out brown with curly hair. I was thinking about your story from the course. Do you remember it?

Matt replies:
Of course I remember it. I had to read it to the whole class.

Ashley continues:
It's the same problem only it's real this time.

Matt replies:
Same solution except the part about the nanny. That part would never work. The part about the sperm and the royal baby is the best aspect of the solution. Do you remember that?

Ashley continues:
Yes, I do. The baby satisfies the continuity of the royal progression.

Matt replies:
That's it. I don't think I can do any better.

Ashley continues:
How do I get a surrogate mother?

Matt replies:
Sorry, I can't help you with that. Wait. I have an idea. I think I have a possible solution.

Ashley continues:
Well, what is it?

Matt replies:
I have to check first. I'll message you back as soon as I find out. Don't worry, we can find a way. I tell you what. I'll message you back tomorrow at about this time. OK?

Ashley continues:
Matt, do you think someone will read our messages?

Matt replies:
Don't worry about it. We are using iMessage so that our messages go through Apple servers and do not get into the cellular system. Apple encrypts the messages, so there is a very good chance that no one can read our communications.

Ashley continues:
Thanks Matt. You're the best.

Matt replies:
No, you are the best.

Matt called Grandfather Miller to explain the problem, but he wasn't in his office. That afternoon just before quitting time, Grandfather calls back. Matt explains the problem to him and he jumps at the idea. He had been searching for a good problem to solve. When Matt asked about the surrogate mother, the Grandfather just treated it as an open item – just another minor problem to be solved. But to Matt's surprise, he says he would take care of it. There was only one catch. Ashley has to send a couple of people to the states to meet with him to insure that this was a bona fide problem and not some boondoggle. Also, he says, "We need some assurance that if we set up a solution, they will really do it. This is definitely not a training exercise." Matt accepts the conditions and thanks his Grandfather profusely.

The next day at the appointed time Matt initiates a message session with Ashley.

Initial message from Matt:
Hi Ashley, I have good news for you. We have a solution.

Ashley replies:
I was just sitting at my computer hoping you would send me a message.

Matt continues:
My Grandfather, the one you have heard about, has taken a liking to your problem and said he would take care of it. When he says he will do something, that should be interpreted to mean that he sees through to a solution, and he will actually do it. There are no conditions on your part or any of your devotees, just do exactly what he says to do.

Ashley replies:
Is this really true? You are kidding me.

Matt continues:
I guarantee to you that it is true.

Ashley replies:
Then, what should I do?

Matt continues:
Tell me the names of your associates so I can set up an appointment for them to come to my office. I will reiterate the conditions and take them to my Grandfather, who will cover everything down to smallest detail. Once the solution is underway, you have only to do what is planned. When I say you, I mean you and the associates who will give you assistance, including the lucky Prince.

Ashley replies:
My friend is August Getraub, who worked with me at the Bon Chic that you probably don't know about, and his associate is Pamela Givens, who is a press agent. I will

talk to them about their schedule and send you a date and time. I guarantee to you that they are dependable and that you can trust them. Thank you very much Matt, you are the real best.

Matt continues:
Ashley, it is a distinct pleasure to work with you and good luck with your future endeavors.

Ashley is thrilled beyond words and wishes she could tell someone about her good fortune. Prince Michael would surely be back soon.

SIXTEEN

THE GENERAL GETS A CALL

Almost like a coincidence, the General gets a call on his satellite Phone.

"Buzz, what a coincidence. I was going to call you. How are you?"

"I'm doing great; the British Security System (BSS) is quite interesting. Of course, not like the stuff we did to help win the war. How are you and why did you call me?"

"It's that situation with that American Ashley Wilson and your Prince Michael. Something has come up."

"That's the subject of interest around here in London," replied Buzz, the General's former wing mate in World War II. They were P-51 flying buddies. "The media and the paparazzi have gone crazy. We got an intercept of messages between your boy Matt and our Duchess to come Nicole Wilson. That's what that Ashley now calls herself. They haven't even been married and people are worked up about the babies. This is serious business here."

"That's why I called Buzz. That Ashley is worked up and contacted Matt. She's supposed to be biracial, and that's the issue."

"She's not biracial Les, and I know women. She doesn't have the ears, nose, read end, or finger nails of a black person. At least one of them comes through. That DNA business can't hide everything. We've seen hundreds of women in our military days. I'll bet a trip to Hawaii on it."

"You've got a bet on that Buzz, even though I agree with you. How do you think we should be proceed?"

"You've got to get her, and maybe even Michael, and the Queen in the States. This place is a boiling pot."

"I've got it," said the General. "The secret honeymoon. I thought of the babies shower, but that's too late to be credible."

"You've got it," replied Buzz. "Now to the reason I called. The Royalty has a terrible problem with bookkeeping and someone is charging large amounts. It's all secret so we, that is the BSS, recommend an outside agency. I recommended you and Matt, and she bought it. Can you get here next week? No more that 4 days max."

"Get us a schedule and we will be there, and Buzz, it will be gratis."

SEVENTEEN

ASHLEY AND HER SOLUTION

Two days later, Ashley and August met for lunch in the Pub Around the Corner. Ashley was jubilant. "We have a solution." said Ashley. Michael would like to go with the first alternative, and I agree totally. I really don't want to be pregnant, and he does not want to be involved with all of the biracial amplifications of a baby at this time. I sent a message to my friend from university days and he said that it could be done. He even said very strongly that it would be done, and all we have to do is follow their procedures. He said that his grandfather agreed to take care of it. Apparently, they like the idea that the royal heritage would be preserved. That's my opinion, not theirs. There are a few little things to do and the first is to go there and meet with the grandfather. He is the gentleman with the airplane who was a general in the army."

"It sounds too good to be true," said August. "Are you sure that your message to your friend was secure. You know we have an ever vigilant government?"

"He said we were using iMessage and that Apple encrypts the messages." "Well, if says so, I suppose it's true. That's not my area." answered August. "Maybe it's only true in the U.S."

"He, the Grandfather, says that someone has to come there to get the details. It isn't much to do. He needs to make sure that things are legit on our end." replied Ashley.

"What about on his end? How do we find out that things are okay on his end?" asked August.

"We have to find out when we go there." said Ashley.

"You can't go. The paparazzi would have a field day. It's the same with Michael. I'm thinking that you would like me to do it."

"I was thinking you would might agree to do it. I could make the arrangements and perhaps even get you some money for you heroic efforts." replied Ashley. "By the way, could you take your friend Pamela, it would look better to our royal watchers," said Ashley.

"Forget the money. Can you just get us travel expenses and first class fares? Pamela would love to go. She really enjoys the States and would like to live there." said August.

"I'll have a diplomatic pouch delivered to your residence that contains everything you will need for your trip to the States. You should use your own passports and travel at your leisure, as long as leisure is interpreted to mean as soon as possible." stated Ashley.

"Now, please tell me about just what I'm getting involved with." remarked August "especially the following."

August continued for a few minutes. "I need the contact that you speak of. Especially the one that wrote the story that this adventure is based on. What is his name and where does he live? If he's a professor, then what is his university and where is it? He sounds like a regular fellow to write such a screwy story. I'm hoping that he is not one that worries about things, especially the fine points of law."

Ashley answered. "I've kind of lost track of him professionally, but I will give as much detailed information as I can in the diplomatic pouch that you will receive. The sperm bank should not be a problem and can be taken care of by one of our royal helpers. You do know that we have people that will help with just about everything you can think of. They are pledged to secrecy. You're going to have to arrange for the surrogate mother and the fast transportation of the sperm sample. I don't think we can arrange those two things from this end. I don't exactly know about the sperm transportation and how the sperm meets up with the airplane – that is, the fast transportation. As you can tell, we do have some resources and know how to use them. We're not exactly busy with all the help, so we have ample time to work things out."

"What about the contact. Is he reliable? Can we count on him to keep his mouth shut? asked August. "Does he have good friends? Does he need money? What about his family?"

"Well, I don't know much about him," replied Ashley. "He's very studious. Does his math homework every night. Doesn't seem to worry about anything. He once said to me that it's all about statistics. His favorite expression is, 'In the long run, things will turn out just fine, so why worry about them.' His parents are well to do and his grandfather seems to be rich and a real nice person. My friend belonged to a fraternity and lived in a fraternity house. He said that living in a frat house was more economical than paying the high fees for university room and board. He didn't have much money – at least when he was a student – but if he wanted something or to do something, he was sure his parents would pay for it. He said he never asked for anything. I once met his Grandfather at our graduation dinner at an expensive restaurant and he just looked at me. Maybe that's how army generals always act. Who knows."

"He sounds like a good contact, but I wonder about his ability to get a surrogate mother," said August. "She has to be the right age and willing to give up the baby. I don't think this is so easy. She has to be good-looking, like you are, but also the right ethnicity. What about the grandfather?"

"All I know about him is that he was in World War II, in the Army Air Corps, flew planes, and got to be a general officer. He seems to know just about everyone important in the U.S., has a very rich polling – like political polling – company, and does unusual things to help people."

"Like what?"

"To start off, he owns a plane, a big one, but never flies it himself. It is used to transport people in need. He paid for flying lessons for my friend Matthew Miller, who is his grandson. He wants Matthew to be able to land a plane. Apparently, the Grandfather was in a situation in the war where he was in a plane and the pilot and co-pilot got shot and he was able to land the plane and save a whole bunch of soldiers. He got a hero's medal for it. He does unusual things to help people, but doesn't charge it to his company, but pays for it out of his own pocket. Matthew says he tries to be 'squeaky clean'."

"That could be good or bad."

"I don't exactly know what you mean by that remark, but I'm pretty sure you will find out," said Ashley.

Ashley and August had run out of words. They finished their lunch and left individually.

Two days later, a diplomatic pouch was delivered to August's temporary residence. It contained destination information, reference data on Matthew Miller, two open-ended round trip first-class airline passes to the U.S., five thousand dollars in travel money, two American Express credit cards, and a brief note stating that August Getraub should be accompanied by a female companion, preferably Pamela Givens, and intent of the female passenger was to avoid unwanted attention. Also included were two financially secure envelopes, each of which contained five thousand dollars, and labeled Unrecorded Tax-Free Stipend. The travelers were reminded to use their own passports.

EIGHTEEN

THE GENERAL AND MAT GO TO LONDON

The General informed Buzz Bunday that he and Matt would arrive at the London City Airport on Wednesday in the afternoon and sleep on the plane. They would need transportation to the palace at approximately 8:30 am on Thursday. All other arrangements are left as open items to be addressed after meeting with the Queen.

On Thursday morning, the following notice with a green border appeared at the palace gate:

* * * *

Her Royal Highness the Queen Announces the Following Visitors to the royal monarchy:

General Les Miller, PhD, United States Army Air Force
Matthew Miller, PhD, distinguished Mathematician

The team will be assisting the Royal Family in the operation of the United Kingdom. The visit of these guests is a distinct honor to the Royal Family.

* * * * *

Sharply at 9:00 am, the two visitors were ushered into the Queen's suite. She was dressed in a bright green dress with suitable jewelry. The visitors were dressed in black suits, white shirts, and black ties. The visitors offered a bow, and the Queen waved it off with a request that they be seated. The Queen was very sophisticated and comfortable with her position as leader of the monarchy.

General Les Miller looked at the Queen, the Queen looked at the General, and both remarked at exactly the same time, "Do I know you?"

The Queen and the General gave each other a big American hug, and the Queen said to the General, "I can still taste that chocolate bar that you gave me on that forlorn road during the war. I was so hungry. I saved the nylons that you gave me and still have them."

The General replied, "When I saw you on that lonely road, I thought you were the prettiest girl I had ever seen. I still do."

Matt looked at the two of them in awe. Here was a Queen and a General behaving like a couple of college students. He would eventually find out, informally, that she also had a PhD that hardly anyone knew about.

The couple began to discuss their lives, since that first meeting. The queen mentioned that her father was the King and she inherited the throne. The Queen, whose nickname was 'Kitty', was busy as a representative of the people and made appearances on about 300 days in a calendar year. Management of the monarchy's finances was indeed a tedious challenge that never eased up. The General mentioned that he was a career Army officer and pilot and was certified as a fighter pilot and as a multi-engine bomber pilot. He also mentioned the fortunate events that facilitated his promotion to general officer.

The Queen also mentioned a downside of being Royalty. By the royal decree, no one is supposed to touch the King or Queen. For her, other than her husband who passed away recently, no person had touched her since her encounter with the General on that muddy road during the war.

The General said, "That is indeed an unfortunate circumstance, and I guarantee you that I will not abstain from giving you an occasional American hug – but not in public.

The Queen initiated the business aspects of their meeting, "Someone, we do not know who, is transferring funds from several royal accounts. We don't know who that is because there are ample funds for every royal's needs and desires. We found out about the situation from the Royal Auditor who noticed that the receiver of the transferred funds was the same numbered account. We initiated a search for the person requesting the bank transfer and it turned out to be my daughter, Princess Amelia. The Royal Auditor asked her about the bank transfer, and she indicated that it must be a mistake. She said she had not ordered any of them. There is an element of trust among royalty in that one person does not question another's integrity. I did not want to bring in the police or security services since they have a tendency to entertain the media with just about everything, resulting in a royal scandal. We would like to avoid a major scandal for any reason."

"What are the amounts of the bank transfers and how often do they occur?" asked the General.

"I can get that information for you," answered the Queen. "I also have the numbered account number right here."

"Do you have a general record of all financial transactions that occur – something like a ledger?" asked the General.

"We don't have anything like that," said the Queen. "We pay no taxes, have no driving licenses, and require no identification of any sort, such as a passport. We have no need to save information."

"It is remarkable that you have a closed society, as you have in the royalty, but in this case, it is counter-productive," said the General. "That is precisely why we have Dr. Matt Miller with us. There are methods for keeping track of any such incidents, and Matt can set it up for you."

"Well, okay then," said the Queen. "I suspect that we need something like that."

"We can and will take care of both problems. I will need access to your Royal Auditor," stated the General. "Matt will take care of the operational situation. I can guarantee to you that we will be practically transparent. Matt will need access to the auditor and your data processing people. I think we can wrap this up in 4 days and at most a week."

The Queen was pleased, and the General could conceptualize a way of investigating and eliminating the bank transfer problem. Matt was awed and impressed with his grandfather, like never before.

* * * * *

After returning to London from Zürich with the financial problem solved, the General scheduled a meeting with the Queen on Monday morning. The Queen responded immediately, confirming the appointment.

The next morning the General woke up early to another cold and dismal day. He figured they would be out of there on Wednesday. The General entered the Queen's suite and attempted to render the necessary bow but she waved it off, as usual.

The General gave the results of the solution in Zürich, and the Queen listened politely. At the conclusion, the Queen thanked the General for a job well done and then issued a conclusion that surprised the General but gave him some insight as to how the Royalty worked.

All she said was, "I am pleased to announce that Princess Amelia has been assigned to the position of Royal Deputy to the British Ambassador in Australia. She left by private plane on Saturday night after the events in Switzerland. Since I run this operation out of London and have supreme power, I made a quick decision. There will be no more surprise expenditures under my watch."

"Do you mean that you knew that Princess Amelia was the source of the problem all along?" asked the General.

"No, I did not, but I had my suspicions. The death of her ex-husband and your computer results in Zürich confirmed everything. You must remember that in the system of British Royalty, the monarch is the supreme leader."

The General responded, "I am surprised but pleased at your success."

"And now, one more thing," said the Queen. "Would you take me on a date tomorrow? I know this is common among Americans, but not for Royalty."

"I would enjoy doing that. Would you like me to make a plan for the day?" asked the General.

"I would be pleased if you did so," responded the Queen.

That evening, the General discussed the situation with Matt, and agreed that tomorrow would render a good opportunity to discuss Ashley and Michael's apparent problem.

NINETEEN

THE GENERAL AND THE QUEEN DISCUESS IMPORTANT STUFF

Bright and early the next morning – and it was a beautiful sunny day – the Queen and the General set off on their date. They both dressed in plain clothes so as not to be recognized and were driven by a chauffeur in a plain English vehicle. The first stop was Harrods, where they looked at goods on each and every floor. The Queen remarked several time, "I can hardly believe that this is how people really shop and live. It is wonderful."

The General bought the Queen a beautiful black ball point pen with the name 'Harrods' printed in gold on the side. The Queen looked at the General with a twinkle in her eyes and said they were not allowed to accept gifts from English people, but the rule said nothing about Americans. The couple spent hours at Harrods, and no one recognized them.

The next stop was the bar at the Ritz hotel. An end booth was reserved so that they could gaze out at the other patrons.

The Queen had an American martini, and the General had a single malt scotch. They both lingered over their drink and talked about the differences between royalty and the normal citizen.

"Are you free to discuss the situation concerning Ashley and Michael?" asked the General.

"I can do what I please and addressed the situation with the media and the paparazzi on several occasions. I have a lot of things to which I have to take into consideration. All I want is that Ashley and Michael are happy and the monarchy does experience any operational damage because of the situation."

"I believe that I can help you," replied the General, "and I am pleased to say that it will definitely involve you, if you so desire. It involves an unusual gift for Ashley and Michael and a public relations opportunity for you."

"I would love to hear about it," replied the Queen. "It is not often that anything interesting and exciting happens around here."

"I am offering two things: a honeymoon vacation for Ashley and Michael in Hawaii, and an invitation for you to visit my fine residence, along with your traveling party, and have an opportunity to solve the apparent problem that Ashley and Michael apparently have."

"I am interested," answered the Queen. "When would this opportunity take place?"

"It would take place directly after the wedding and its festivities. Ashley, Michael, you, and your entourage will travel to the United States as my guest at my fine residence. We will have a dinner at my fine restaurant named the

Green Room, and they will proceed forthwith to Hawaii. You and your traveling guests will view the United States as my guest. You and I and appropriate personnel will iron out the situation to the benefit of the monarch and the newly wedded couple. You may return to London together or separately as you please. The entire trip will be of no expense to you or the monarchy. I and my team will take care of all of the details."

"I have to think about it, but the offer is very tempting," replies the Queen. "I will let you know in the morning before you and Matt return to the states."

The last stop was Simpson's on the Strand, where they each had a special roast beef dinner with treacle pudding for dessert. They were both very quiet on the ride back to the palace.

The Queen said, "This was the best day of my life. Thank you." She gave the General a sophisticated kiss. "It is quite amazing that I could go for one whole day and be recognized by no one."

The day with the Queen was over.

*   *   *   *   *

Matt finished his work during the next day, and the General and Matt flew back to the States. There was little conversation on the long ride home. They were successful and life was good.

The Queen called the General and said that she would accept the offer.

TWENTY

AUGUST AND PAMELA VISIT THE STATES

Exactly one week later, August made a light knock on the open door of Dr. Matthew Miller's office in the Mathematics Building. August and Pamela stood in the hallway in an intense state of anticipation. The light knock engendered a brief, "Please go in and take a seat." The speaker was behind them. "The receptionist downstairs alerted me and here I am. I'm Matt Miller."

The office was spacious and appointed with a large wooden desk, credenza, executive office chair, two side chairs, a green sofa, a coffee table, and two green occasional chairs. "Thanks for visiting us," said Miller, "Would you like a cup of coffee. I have one of those automatic machines just waiting for a customer."

"No, thank you," the visitors replied in union."

"How can I help you?" asked Miller.

"I think I should explain who we are and why we are here." answered August. "You probably don't know that."

Miller smiled. "Oh, but I do. You are August and she is Pamela. You are German and spend your working time between the U.S. and Europe. She is British and is just getting started with a promising career in public relations. You are here on behalf of Ashley Wilson." Miller said.

"How in the world do you know that?" asked Pamela.

"Ashley and I exchanged messages a few days ago. Ashley briefly described the situation. I suspect it is a problem of sorts and solving problems is what I do." added Miller.

Miller was tall, handsome, and athletic looking. He had that smile that makes all problems immediately disappear. He continued, "I also know additional facts, but don't let them disturb you. I know what flight you were on, the type of aircraft, the seats and class of the flight, where you stayed yesterday night, and the fact that you had separate rooms. I even know the number of the taxi that you took to the campus and to this building. In fact, I know everything."

"Is this surveillance you are performing legal and does everyone know about it in this country?" asked August.

Miller smiled again and leaned back in one of the green chairs. "This project that provides surveillance for the protection of Americans is not a secret, but it is generally unknown, because most people are too busy or lazy to look into it. My grandfather, who owns and runs a successful political polling company, has a contract with the authorities to develop a system to protect the citizens from terrorism. He does this as a subsidiary. I know about analytics and work for it as a consultant. I'm quite busy as I teach three courses, work on my math research projects, and also work on the security system. I have a computer with access to the system in a secure room in my home. When I got the message from Ashley, I put a look-see on you. That's a nice way of not having to use the word 'trace' that is loaded with negative connotations."

"Then you know why we are here," said August.

"Yes, I do," answered Miller. "I know the problem, that's all. I approached my grandfather and he bought me into the challenge in a few minutes. We need to know the parties we are dealing with. That is specifically why you are here. You will meet him, and you will like him. He has experience being trustworthy. He even looks like someone you can trust. That is very important in this kind of operation. I have to tell you, though, that he is a fast talker and a person who makes fast decisions. He is open to suggestions and is a kind man. Here is something about him. He was a P-51 Mustang pilot during World War II. He completed 25 sorties and was transferred out of his wing. That number is the limit. He then trained for and was certified as a B-29 pilot, and when the B-52 came along, he piloted that also. He subsequently moved into administration and retired from the newly formed Air Force as a Major General. He formed a successful political polling company and then un-retired and is involved in several governmental projects. He strongly believes in the concept of 'need to know' so I don't know much about that stuff. He personally owns a Gulfstream 650 airplane but doesn't fly it as a pilot, only as a passenger. He thinks that a surrogate mother can be found and proposes a woman in her late twenties with middle European characteristics. He thinks the woman should be healthy, in good shape, and not be exceptionally beautiful. He initially thought that the actual mother could be the nanny, and that is why he thought about beauty. Then he changed his mind about the nanny and concluded that it is not in the problem domain. That will be your problem, if it is in fact a problem. You may desire not to have a nanny."

"He knows influential people all over the world, but feels the plan should be orchestrated from the United States, because he knows how things work. He thinks that any problems that could arise will be on your end."

"He seems to know a lot more about this project than I would have predicted," said August.

Miller was quick to answer. "Ashley gave a thorough description of their plans. It's very possible that they have decided things that even you and Pamela don't know, and there are probably things that you and Pamela know that I don't know. The 'need to know' concept is more powerful than most people think it is."

"So August and I are messengers, at best," said Pamela.

"That's likely the case at this stage of the project," said Miller. "Having people involved is more secure and more legitimate. If you two were not here, we would not know if it all was real or a computer-generated scenario."

"Should we conclude that everything – that is, all of the details – has been decided upon?"

"No, not at all. We are providing only the framework for the operation. How the framework is used is dependent upon what Ashley and Prince Michael want to achieve. We provide only the elements and the principles supply the glue that tie the elements together. It is exactly the same as how modern business and the military operate. The suppliers develop the equipment, buildings, ammunition, and other artifacts to the user group. If a subsequent operation is successful, then the user gets all the rewards; if the operation is unsuccessful, then it is unfortunately the supplier that gets the bad reputation."

"Then your part has already been decided?" asked Pamela.

"The answer is yes, but it doesn't end with me. You will meet with the General at 2:00 this afternoon when he will provide the parameters of the operation. Remember that the 'need to know' principle applies. I will not need to know what information is provided to you," answered Miller, "and I will not be present in your meeting."

"One more topic," continued Miller. "The General was a general officer in the U.S. Air Force, but he isn't now. He is an ordinary citizen of the United States, just like I am. His name is Leslie Miller. We have the same last name for obvious reasons. He is a very distinguished person who has been awarded medals, citations, and promotions. So we don't call him Leslie or Miller or even grandfather. He is the General. I look like him, again for obvious reasons. He's not sensitive and is exceptionally easy to get along with. I think that he is quite busy now and has a lot of people with which to deal, so he will not spend much time with you. But remember this. If he says that he will do something, then he will for sure do it. He has often said to me the following, 'If I say I'll do something, then consider it done.' I have a class in a few minutes. It is a course on Category Theory and the students are PhD candidates. I don't want to be late.

Please meet me in the lobby at 1:30 and we'll walk to his office. Another thing, if he offers you coffee, don't take it. He thinks it is a crutch – a sign of weakness."

August and Pamela just looked at each other. The meeting was over. Professor Miller dashed out to his classroom. As they left the room, August said to Pamela, "This sure isn't like home. So there aren't any coffee drinkers around. They must drink bourbon. I think we should be called the Bourbonnais."

Pamela just chuckled.

TWENTY ONE

BREAKTIME

Pamela and August wandered downstairs to the lobby and asked the receptionist for the location of the toilet and where they could get a bite to eat. She appeared to be doing her homework. She directed them to the restroom facilities, after giving a smile hearing the word 'toilet.' She also pointed to the snack room that included a sandwich machine and a soft drink dispenser. "Everything is free here," she said, "we're rich." Those were her only words.

August murmured a few words under his breath, "I wonder what she is studying. It looks like some ancient language."

"It might be math," Pamela said, "but not any kind of math that I've ever seen. I hope the General doesn't expect us to know the new kind of the new math. If so, we're in big trouble."

"Miller said the General is easy to get along with. Remember that."

Neither Pamela nor August were hungry because of the tension created with having to meet the General. Both had a free fruit drink and just sat in a comfortable corner trying to relax.

August was the first to speak. "I don't understand this country. Here we are in this extravagant building with hardly anyone doing anything. How can they afford it?"

"Rich people donate money to the university and it is tax deductible." answered Pamela. "Then the university puts their name on the building. This building is named Carnegie Hall. I suppose the name helps the students to know where to go. This is a private university and government money is not used. In my country, the government pays for everything."

It's the same in Germany." said August. "I suppose there are public universities here as well."

"I would like to live here." said Pamela, "I have looked up on the Internet practically everything I could think of. There are about 4,200 to 4,300 universities in the US, but I never found the breakdown between public and private. This is a very large country, and for most people, a university degree helps to get a good job. Business is big here. I've heard that the business of the University is business."

"I'm not sure what that means," answered August.

Time passed quickly. At 1:35, Matthew Miller appeared. He was calm, cool, and collected.

Sorry I'm late," he said. "We had a student who has an issue with a mathematical proof he was working on. If we move along, we can make it by 2:00. It's only a short walk. No one is ever late for a meeting with the General."

Pamela and August just looked at each other, and Matthew took off like a shot.

TWENTY TWO

MEETING WITH THE GENERAL

Matthew Miller left Pamela and August off at the General's door. He advised them in route that his 'need to know' was finished and that meeting with them was a distinct pleasure.

The General ushered Pamela and August into his office. It was small, neat, and overlooked a man-made lagoon. The General's desktop was free of everything except two smartphones; one was black and the other was red. The contents of the room were exactly the same as Matt's office, down to the green sofa and green occasional chairs.

"Please be seated," said the General. "My name is Leslie Miller, and I work at this company.

Please make yourselves comfortable. Would either of you like coffee?" Both Pamela and August indicated that they did not.

The General continued. "I know of your situation and why you are here. We operate at the secret level here, so do not take notes and please tell no one of this meeting with the exception of Ashley Wilson and Prince Michael. Please make no telephone calls on the subject and do not transmit any information to writing. Do not use the Internet or electronic mail for communication on the subject of this meeting. You should act as you normally do with family, friends, and business associates. Are there any questions so far?"

Both Pamela and August indicated no.

The General continued. "We are committed to help you and guarantee that our end of the operation will be executed to your satisfaction. There will be no mistakes. In the process, you and your associates will violate no U.S. laws and you will incur no financial liability whatsoever. As things proceed, we will need to communicate and we will set up procedures for doing so. Okay so far?"

Pamela and August indicated in the affirmative.

The General again continued. "We respect the sovereign rights of your country and will endeavor to continue the royal biological lineage. Accordingly, we need a sperm sample from Prince Michael, and we understand from the communication from Ashley Wilson that a sperm sample has already been taken and stored in a sperm bank. Also, Asley's eggs have been stored as well. The latter is a matter of national policy and not specifically a part of this operation. We have an airplane at our disposal that will pick up said sperm and egg sample at a predetermined location and transport it to a location in the U.S. with which to fertilize the surrogate mother. After the surrogate fetus has matured to term, we will move the surrogate baby to your country to support the planned pregnancy of Ashley Wilson."

"The specific location for pick up will be a small military airport north of the city. Prince Michael, through his military service, knows of this airfield and has flown in and out of it. After arrival, the airplane will be parked at a location in the northeast corner far away from the terminal operation area. The airport is no longer used for military travel."

"We need to fertilize the egg from the surrogate mother, so we need to know when to do so. A member of your team will communicate to my office when the sperm will be available at said airfield and we will arrange to have it picked up. The transfer should take place as soon as possible. The surrogate mother will be fertilized after the marriage of Ashley Wilson and Prince Michael, and a reasonable date should be established. As a courtesy to the surrogate mother, some advanced notice should be given. A suitable date should take the form, 'Ninety-six hours after the marriage of Ashley Wilson and Prince Michael'. We will fertilize the mother and inform you accordingly."

"The gestation period for humans is 280 days plus or minus 10 days. We will inform you when the surrogate mother goes into labor and when the baby is born. We will deliver the newborn baby to the same spot in the airfield. We will plan on transferring the baby to you forty-eight hours after birth. You will be informed of estimated time of arrival down to a five- minute interval. The aircraft will be equipped with all necessary medical equipment. A trained medical doctor and a pediatric nurse will accompany the baby. At your end, the pick up and delivery of the newborn baby to the intended place of birth should mirror the environment used for the air transport. That means a suitable vehicle, all necessary equipment, and trained personnel. The description I have just given supports Ashley Wilson's plan for a surrogate birth. The activity on your end must support that objective. Now I think it is time for a short break."

"Are we supposed to remember all of the information you have given us?" asked Pamela.

"The answer is yes. Most of it is common sense. Our end is straightforward. Your end is a little more complicated and it has still to be worked out. For example, is it to be a home birth or a hospital birth? As I suggested, let's take a break." The General added.

The General hesitated for a few seconds and said, "I could use a drink of water. I'll ask for water and some soft drinks. I'm used to operating in this manner, but the two of you probably are not." The General stood and stretched. For an older gentleman, he was in fine shape. He cut a handsome figure and as Miller mentioned, they looked alike.

The General was proud of the facilities. "I'll tell you about the complex we have here. All of this was a low-lying area and we developed a plan for flooding. We built a set of connected lagoons to hold surface water, so when flooding occurs, the water is equitably distributed between the lagoons. The area in-between was filled with a substantial combination of clay and sand, called loam, and topsoil. Appropriate vegetation makes it look like a park area."

An elderly lady brought in bottled water and various drinks and juices. Pamela and August reloaded. Everything was going to be okay.

The General continued. "I am particularly concerned with the method of communication. I suggest that you use a diplomatic pouch. To send information to me, place the information in a diplomatic pouch, address it to Richard Hargrove and take it to the U.S. Embassy in whatever city you reside. Richard Hargrove is code name. It will be delivered to me in less than twenty- four hours. When I want to send information to you, I will place it in a similar pouch and have it transported to the same U.S. Embassy. You will be notified of said pouch and you must pick it up there. I will use the expertise of Dr. Matthew Miller, the professor that you met, for sending messages via iMessage when the need arises."

"I will advise you on the vehicles you use for transferring items between us. You should use a readily recognizable vehicle such as a dark blue SUV that will not engender unwanted attention. The airplane will be a Gulfstream 650 that I own. The personnel involved will work for me on this project, although they will have other full-time jobs. The doctors will know how to handle sperms and preserve them, and they will also have great knowledge of taking care of babies. Okay so far?"

August and Pamela looked awestruck. The General looked at them and recognized it immediately. He continued. "You look like you think that this endeavor can't possibly work. I guarantee that it is foolproof, and it will work perfectly. Governmental agencies and large corporations do these kinds of operations on a routine basis. How do you think that corporations such as Apple can conceptualize, design, manufacture and outsource, assemble, and market millions of smartphones, for example, in almost complete secrecy? We would like to have Ashley to come to the states for a baby shower. She should be accompanied by a person involved with the deception, such as you August. We will make a contact with you and Ashley to confirm that the development of the surrogate baby is progressing as planned. The news media will provide the information on the shower for our convenience."

"Now we have to discuss your end of the birth of the royal baby. Ashley and Prince Michael are completely free to do what they want to do." The General said. "Of course, the framework we have developed supports the option of producing no baby at your end and faking the pregnancy. That would be done through the use of progressively larger pad that emulate the familiar baby bump. When the fully mature surrogate baby is received on your end, the pads are removed and a birth is presented. We recommend this option. Ashley could also achieve pregnancy and then replace the 'still born baby' with the surrogate form. We do not recommend this option or other similar options. Such as, if the baby produced is unsatisfactory, then and only then, replace it. Well, this is the end of the story. By the way, Richard Hargrove is a fictitious name; no Richard Hargrove exists. That is the only item you have to remember."

The General stood up and smiled and his visitors relaxed. He was so assured that there was no doubt the operation would succeed. In that regard, he was like his grandson Matt Miller. "There is a car downstairs with a driver. He will be at your disposal. There is a splendid complimentary dinner reserved for your pleasure this evening. It completely prepaid. Actually, I own the establishment and its name is *The Green Room*. I recommend the filet steak."

The General pressed an icon on the black phone and a smartly dressed young lady came in and handed two light green envelopes to him. As Pamela and August left the room, the General handed each of them an envelope. He simply said, "Thank you for your patience."

TWENTY THREE

THE TRIP HOME

On their flight home, Pamela and August compared mental notes. August said, "He must be pretty rich, my envelope contains five thousand in hundred dollar bank notes."

Pamela responded, "Mine did as well. I wish all of life were this easy."

"Actually," said August, "we really didn't do anything. All we've done so far is listen to the Americans and now to report to Ashley and Prince Michael, and I guess we are finished. Do you agree?"

"I think you're absolutely right. I love first-class flights. I think British Airways is the best airline. I'm glad they still use the 747 airplane." When they arrived back home, a luncheon was arranged at the Pub Around the Corner. Ashley and Prince Michael were anxious to receive the results of the trip to the United States.

Ashley was a bit anxious. "Did everything turn out to our satisfaction? You were only gone a few days. How was

Matthew? Was he cordial. What was he doing in life? How does he look?"

Pamela answered, and August looked as though he would prefer to skip the small talk. "The trip went as you planned and we think things are worked out to your satisfaction. Your friend Matthew was friendly, but very serious. He's a professor now and is busy with his courses, his research, and work for his grandfather. He looked good, very handsome, and quite athletic looking. He didn't talk about you, but based upon what he did for you, he must have liked you a lot. He and his grandfather look alike and they call him the General. The grandfather, that is. His real is Leslie Miller."

August broke into Pamela's report. "Your friend Matthew and the General have things worked out and seemed in a hurry with us. I couldn't figure out if they really didn't want to work with us or they were very busy. Perhaps, they are doing too much for people that don't want to do anything for themselves. Then again, they didn't know us. But, the General did say that we wouldn't be breaking any U.S. laws. Here is my summary. We have to get for them a sperm and egg sample, and when you do, you have to inform them of when they can pick it up at an airport in the General's airplane – a Gulfstream. The airport is an unused military base north of here that the General said Prince Michael would know about."

"I do," said Prince Michael. "I know about all of the bases in England. Remember, I was formerly a fighter pilot."

"You have to place the date and time in a diplomatic dispatch pouch and leave it at the U.S. Embassy addressed to a Richard Hargrove." continued August "It is a code name. Remember, you can change the plan. They are only providing a service."

"Well it sounds to me that they are doing more, much more than only providing a service," said Ashley, "They have worked out the whole scenario concerning our problem of having a royal baby. I think it is pretty good. In fact it seems to me to be real good. Personally, I am more than thankful."

August was taken aback by Ashley's support for the Americans. He continued in a subdued fashion. "They will know of your wedding from the news media. They will fertilize a surrogate mother with the sperm ninety-six hours after the wedding – that's four days."

Pamela interrupted August. "That's not exactly true. The ninety-six hours was used only as an example. We have to inform them when we want the surrogate mother fertilized by the diplomatic dispatch pouch, as mentioned previously."

August continued, "They treated the subject of the American nanny as an open item. When the surrogate baby is born, they will wait forty-eight and then bring the baby to you at the same airport. You will informed of the date and time of birth via the same diplomatic route, and the date and time of the delivery to you in the same message. They recommend an identifiable vehicle, such as a large dark blue SUV. You will then transfer the baby to the place of birth, being a home location or a hospital. You, Ashley, and Prince Michael have to work out how and when the details of the birth are presented to the public."

Prince Michael whispered to Ashley, "It sounds like your friend August is not the sharpest knife in the drawer." Ashley replied, "It does sound like it."

"The General covered the case when another scheme was used, such as having a real birth here, and then responding accordingly," said Pamela, "but recommended against it."

Ashley interrupted and said, "I do not have to get pregnant and do not even know if it is possible. We are using the royalty pregnancy scenario because of their need to have offspring. I don't even necessarily agree with that. I'm letting you know that the first option we've discussed is the only one."

"Well, that's it then," said August. "There are other items to discuss, but for now, we have brought you up to date on the progress, so far. Oh, there is one more thing. The General thinks you should have a baby shower in the U.S. so you can meet the surrogate, and that I should escort you. But, we can cover that later."

"Let's have lunch," said the Prince.

TWENTY FOUR

COMPLICATED PREPARATIONS

As planned, undercover arrangements were made by Prince Michael to have his sperm and Ashley's eggs to the airport at an arranged time. The pickup was made with the General's Gulfstream and as far as the parties in the royal wedding were concerned, all systems in the complicated operation were 'go.'

Meanwhile, the American team had some work to do. "Matt," commanded the General, "we have some work to do."

"I'm a busy man, General," answered Matthew Miller, the doer of all deeds in his grandfather's estimation. "I have courses to teach, a paper to write on Category Theory, and some analytics to do for your company."

"We have to find a surrogate mother for that friend of yours," said the General. "We have a deadline. You know that."

"No, I don't. You know that I didn't have a 'need to know" on that solution of yours."

"Now you do. Anyhow, I've heard that classes are over at that so-called university of yours.

Can you get away for a couple of days?"

"Depends upon whether a couple is two days or a couple is a week or more. Also, I would like to remind you that this university is the best in the country if not the world."

"Sorry about the university. I know it is the best," said the General, "How about two days starting this coming Monday. We'll fly out on Sunday evening and return on Tuesday evening, or before."

"Where are we going?" asked Matt.

"I'll tell you Sunday evening, just before we leave. Someone may be listening."

"Why all the secrecy? Those two people that were here know just about everything we do in that regard." Questioned Matt. "I doubt anyone is listening. A knowledgeable person, known as the General, recently told me that satellite phones, at least the kind we use, are secure."

"You win. A car will pick you up at your house at 6 pm."

"I'll be there."

A car stopped at Matt's house at 6 pm on Sunday, as planned. Actually, the vehicle might not really be regarded as a car. It was a black armor plated Mercedes S-Class with run-flat tires and bullet proof glass. The driver was a professional. Matt came out of the house with a light case and the rear right door opened. The General was the first to speak, "Good to see you Matt."

Matt answered, "Good to see you too General. Where are we headed?"

"The airport," answered the General.

"Which one?"

"Our local one. We're taking a helicopter," the General added.

"Actually, I was thinking of the final destination," said Matt.

"I guess I do have to tell you. It's the George Bush Center for Intelligence," said the General.

"Now that's a new one. I've never heard of it," responded Matt.

"That is the new name for the CIA headquarters in Langley, Virginia."

"Well, it will be fun, no matter what the name," said Matt. "I'm overjoyed."

"We have a volunteer that you should meet. As you are the only one that actually knows this Ashley Wilson, the person who would like a surrogate mother," replied the General.

The helicopter took them to a small military airport and then a Cessna took them to Dover Air Force base in New Hampshire, long closed except for government executive travel. From there, they flew to Langley in a private jet. At Langley, they spent the night in a CIA safe house on the CIA campus.

The day starts early at the Bush Center and the appointment with the volunteer was scheduled for 8 am. It was an unusual occurrence at the Bush Center that the personnel department was late with the candidate.

While they waited, Matt had a few questions for the General. "I'm really concerned with our involvement with the CIA in what would appear to be a private matter in another country. I will admit that the key person involved with this case is an American citizen, but all of this secrecy is a bit over the top."

"There's a lot you don't know Matt," said the General. "During the war, many of the officers had unusual roles in the conflict. I was recruited by the OSS to work on covert operations, so that I have a very strong connection to many of the offices. Even though I do not have an official relationship with the CIA, I know many of the key people so that we can work together on diverse projects. People like us help them. There are many others who do the same, and this manner of working together is frequently done. Have you read any of the Daniel Silva novels?"

Matt responded, "Yes I have. I've read all 26 of them, including the last entitled *The Collector*."

"Then you've read about one of his characters named Julian Isherwood who serves the Israeli version of the CIA called the Office as a volunteer helper called a *sayan*. I suspect that's what we are." said the General. "Well, I might as well tell you. Your friend Ashley is a sayan and so is the surrogate mother."

Matt was flabbergasted.

"The basic requirement for the surrogate mother is a normal sized healthy female with dark hair, brown eyes, and middle European skin color. The personnel department has done their job and the mother-to-be is a sweet young lady who has just graduated from the basic CIA school. She been examined by an experienced OB/GYN and she estimated that there was at least a 99.8% chance that she would produce a viable baby. She has a high IQ, a requirement of all recruits. She is no longer an employee of the U.S. government. Her personal expenses are paid by me, and she he gets a notably high stipend for doing this. All of the finances are paid personally paid by me. The U.S. government or anyone else is not involved in the process."

"There is another thing," continued the General. "She offered to play the role of the nanny, in the event that Ashley needs to be extracted from her royal position. I mentioned that was an open item at this point."

"Why are we doing this?" asked Matt. "It is so complicated."

"Only because our government needs and likes information to preserve our safety and to maintain our position as a dominant country in an ever-changing world. Many persons concur with this point of view, including myself, and that is precisely why we try to aid the government when we can. Ashley and the surrogate mother feel the same way."

Matt and General interviewed the young lady and agreed she was suitable for the job.

The General asked her the final question. "Do you agree with the conditions of this assignment and agree to fulfill the requirements of the position to the best of your ability?"

The future surrogate mother responded, "Yes Sir, I do." All the persons in the room smiled. The conditions had been given to the candidate up front, and she had just accepted the position.

The General added several more comments. "The sperm will be inserted, as covered previously in the conditions, within approximately ninety-six hours after the wedding of Ashley Wilson and Prince Michael. We have been advised of this requirement just recently from the bride. Additionally, when your baby is born, it will transported to the royal destination in forty- eight hours. Ashley Wilson and Prince Michael will be the official parents of the baby and all determinations will be their responsibility. They will have a birth registration issued as is the custom."

The surrogate mother's name was suspended and her new name would be Emma Williams, born in Pebble Creek, New Jersey to two teachers who were killed in an auto accident. Emma had graduated from nursing school and just wanted to try something different for a couple of years that would make a difference. In reality, that was the same reason that Ashley agreed to a position as a sayan; she wanted to make a difference.

"Just for your general knowledge, and I know you like to know everything," said the General to Matthew Miller as they left the room, "the roles of the two women are entirely different. Ashley gets no financial support for her role as a princess. Emma has her salary maintained in escrow. When she goes back to work for the United States, she gets the money plus a bonus. If she doesn't come back under the umbrella, she gets nothing. It's a tough world. The difference between the two is that Ashley approached us, and we approached Emma."

The recruitment of the surrogate mother had been completed without difficulty of any sort.

The General and Matthew returned home that evening. A discussion opened up during the flights.

The General started off. "Now that you are a highly educated professional in an important position, you probably should give some attention to national problems. Here is what I have been thinking about. There is a diminishing exchange of practical information between the business world, including government, and the academic community. Unless we do something about it, we could find ourselves as a second-class country. Great things are being done in the business world, but the newly trained academic leaders are not tuned in to them." The General continued, "So here is essentially a snapshot of what I have in mind. Take the College of Business in a traditional university. It is divided into departments, such as management, accounting, and marketing. Of course, there are other departments. At first in the development of the business curriculum, the departments called upon the business and government leaders to teach courses as full time and adjunct faculty, so that the exchange of information on methods and processes proliferated. Then as time progressed, the outside information diminished because the faculty's experience was limited. That's my view of the old fashioned P-H-D concept – piled higher and deeper. So my thinking is that degrees from sub-departments such as management should be developed wherein there could be specialties, such as aerospace management, commodities management, and financial management. The notion of a general specialty, such as business, is very good but it has ballooned into a large monstrosity of information that is possibly outdated. Just an idea Matt, but then again, you do in fact have a specialty that could be what I'm conceptualizing about. Maybe these are just the ramblings of an old man. We are close to our destination, so we continue this at another time when I can listen to you."

"Thanks General."

TWENTY FIVE

THE WEDDING AND THE HONEYMOON

A wedding is always a gala occasion. A royal wedding is a hundred weddings, relatively speaking, jammed into one. There are dinners, parties, and other festivities designed to raise the tempo to a resounding roar. The media go crazy, and the paparazzi go nuts. As mentioned previously, the paparazzi even needed to get new batteries for taking spy photos with their iPhones. The royal wedding of Ashley Wilson and Prince Michael was beyond belief, because people loved her or hated her, but above all, they were genuinely interested. What could be more interesting than an American drama queen and a socially accepted royal prince? All of Prince Michael's polo friends were in attendance with their wives or girlfriends, as the case may be. Ashley's friends were somewhat limited due to the difficulty of Americans entering the royal scene. Hats slanted to the right were the delight of the day. When the bride's long train was finally tucked away, the couple drove away in dramatic fashion in a luxurious limousine.

The Queen conferred the titles of the Duke and Duchess of Bordeaux on the jubilant couple. To many on the street, she was referred to as the Royal Highness Princess of Bordeaux. She was their Princess Ashley.

Then, the Queen announced the surprise of the royal wedding. With the best wishes of her friend and colleague General Les Miller, the newlyweds would be taking a honeymoon trip to Hawaii at his expense, and she, the Queen with her traditional entourage as well as the Duke and Duchess of Bordeaux would be flying the newly built supersonic transport to the states. The newlyweds would continue on to Hawaii for their stay in an exquisite hotel with all of the frills and advantages of the finest hotel that Hawaii could provide. I will be taking a diplomatic trip to the states. We will be returning together.

* * * * *

The trip was heralded throughout the free world. The attendees at the celebration dinner was mind boggling: The Queen, The President and First Lady, the Vice President and Second Lady, the two ambassadors, and as many dignitaries that could fit into the large dining hall. Even the Queen's entourage was invited. What was served? You guessed it. Clear soup, prime filet, baked potato, salad, vegetables, and anything else imaginable. It was a grand dinner, only to be interrupted by the Maitre D, who apologized and mentioned that he had to begin clearing the dishes because of a new

state law. Slowly, it got done. On the way out, the Maitrè
D handed two sheets of paper to the General. The crowd
disbursed and Matt and the General were alone.

Matt asked what the test results were and the General
looked totally bewildered.

"Matt, how did you know?" asked the General

"You under estimate me, Sir," answered Matt. "I ran
through all of he possibilities and that was the only conclusion
I could draw. You gave it away for sure when you did not
respond to the ending of the dinner."

"Both Ashley and Michael are completely clean; they are
both Caucasian, and Ashley must have been adopted."

"I will give the paper to the Queen and let her decide,"
said the General. "But I will notify the physician to halt the
surrogation. It hasn't started yet. We had 96 hours."

* * * * *

The Queen was stressed out, because of all the dignitaries,
and notified her staff that she should not be bothered in any
case. The General was the exception.

"Would you enjoy a small class of our new white wine
Kitty?" asked the General.

"With you Les, of course."

"Once you get settled, I'll meet you in the drawing room,"
said the General. "I could use a little relaxation, myself."

The Queen was there in five minutes and before she
could sit down, the General handed her the two sheets of
paper that had been handed to him.

She had the largest smile that he had scene in many years, and immediately sat down.

"It's your call," said the General. "It's in your domain."

The Queen responded immediately, "Let's go through with the surrogation with Ashley's eggs and Michael's sperms. That's what Ashley would want. She wants a baby and will be a good mother. She just doesn't want to have the baby. Can you take care of that?"

"I'll do that immediately," answered the General. "We will go with Emma Williams, the surrogate mother, as planned."

"Exactly, " said the Queen. "I will tell them now, before they leave for Hawaii in the morning. What we tell the media and the paparazzi is an open item. Will you help me?"

"Of course," replied the General. "Tell Ashley and Michael, and then get some sleep. You look tired."

"Thanks Les, you're the best."

TWENTY SIX

BACK FROM THE HONEYMOON

Ashley and Michael returned and everyone was excited to hear about the trip. Both were upbeat, but then asked to speak confidently to the Queen.

"We have troubles mum," said Prince Michael. "We had to visit a physician while in Hawaii and I am afraid to have to tell you the Ashley has a medical condition. She is expected to have extreme difficulty delivering a baby and she might have to visit a specialist in the continental U.S. She may need a hysterectomy. We should see one immediately."

"I'll take care of it," said the Queen, as cool as a cucumber. "I'll contact the General right away. Be calm and rest. There will be a simple solution. We are in the U.S."

The Queen knocked on the door to the General's study. He was having a coffee with Matt.

"Good morning General and Matt," said the Queen. "I'm sorry to bother you. We have a problem."

"We can handle it," said the General. "That is why we are here."

"Ashley has a medical situation, and I think it should be attended to as soon as possible," said the Queen.

"What kind of problem Your Highness?" asked Matt. "We need to know how to start."

"Perhaps, a hysterectomy," replied the Queen rather hesitantly.

"Mass General," said Matt and the General at the same time.

"I'll take care of it right away," said the General. "Just leave the States today, as planned, and stop in Boston. I'll have a government office take care of the hospital part and the travel arrangements. It will all be of no charge to you."

The Queen left, satisfied by the kind and calm words of the General and Matt.

"She has a delivery channel or canal problem, because she is so small and slender," said Matt. "My sister had the exact same situation. Ashley is young and healthy and could be out of the hospital and headed home the next day. Two days at most. They kept my sister only the night of the procedure. Ashley will not be able to have a baby afterwards."

"That solves the Queen's problem," said the General. "We turn the surrogate back on with Ashley's eggs and Michael's sperms, and the Queen simply tells the media and paparazzi about the hysterectomy and the system will unravel itself on its own. There is no reason to announce anything besides the truth.

TWENTY SEVEN

BACK IN THE STATES

Back in the states, Emma Williams is fertilized with Prince Michael's sperm and Ashley's eggs 96 hours after the wedding. The surrogate mother-to-be was set up in a luxurious apartment in her hometown of Pebble Creek, New Jersey.

It was a comfortable location for the job at hand. To the people at large, Emma's husband was an Air Force officer serving in the Middle East on an extended tour of duty. Fortunately, her sister and brother were available to visit her and tend to her needs. The apartment had all of the facilities necessary for pregnant woman. She visited her OB/GYN regularly.

Emma was in good shape and felt good. She enjoyed being pregnant, since she did not have the niggling problems that some women experience. There was public park nearby, and she thoroughly enjoyed watching young children playing with their parents.

Emma was pleased that she had accepted the position of nanny, because she would be with the baby that she carried for nine months. Her son or daughter would live in royalty for her whole life. The only thing better than that would be to be a princess. In fact, she could actually end up being a real life princess.

There was another key element. Her expected salary as a nanny was $90,000 per year, and she would have no expenses. She also expected her government salary that would be held in escrow. With that much money, she should be able to go back to college to get her master's degree and possible even her doctorate. Sometimes the cards just fell into place when a person least expected them to. She liked people but wasn't so sure that being a nurse was the best way to work with them.

Then she had an idea that she thought was pretty good. Why not record her experiences and thoughts about being a nanny into a diary, and use it afterwards to write a book about various aspects of child care, or even a relevant novel. Then she thought 'I'd better start this diary of experiences right from the being, or I will never do it.'

Emma had liked to walk before the position of surrogate came up. Her OB/GYN told her that regular walk would help with her pregnancy and eventual birth. She tried to walk 10,000 steps every day, and found that was easily achievable.

Life was good for Emma Williams.

TWENTY EIGHT

PLANNING FOR THE BABY SHOWER

A baby shower is a convenient means of giving presents to an expectant mother. It is commonplace in the United States and not so much in Europe and the British Isles. For the royalty, it is taboo. Why would a member of the royalty need a baby shower when they always have everything they need?

Ashley liked the idea of a baby shower in the States. She could see her friends, most of whom were established individuals on stage, TV, and in the movies. She also thought she wouldn't mind some American food. The queen had some severe dietary restrictions with which she didn't always agree. In the States, she didn't mind if people looked at her, in fact, she liked it. They did not often see a duchess. But in the royal community, it was a different story altogether.

Ashley called August and arranged a meeting at the Pub Around the Corner. He was happy to comply. A free lunch in London was nothing to sneeze at. Prices are high.

"It's good to see you August," said Ashley. "It's a little tedious up there in the stables. They watch me all of the time and always want to help me. I have no control over the watchers. They call it security."

"That's the price you have to pay to be royalty," answered August. "It will get better as they get used to you, but as of now, you are still an American. They probably think you are going to steal the crown jewels, whatever they and wherever they are. Just kidding."

That is precisely the reason I wanted this meeting," said Ashley. "Can we go ahead with the baby shower in the States? It was mentioned to me by the General. I'm sure you will never forget him."

"Sure, I'll set it up for whenever you would like," said August. "Give me a list of the attendees and either a phone number or email address for each one and when you would like it, and I will set it all up. Give me the hotel you would prefer, or perhaps, you know of a person who would host it."

"Here it all is," exclaimed Ashley with a proud look on her face. "I made it up before I came here. I can't travel alone. It's a rule, and Prince Michael doesn't want to go to the States. So you are the man to do the job."

"It's just not that easy now that you are a member of the royal family," said August. "You have an entourage that includes people from the royal travel group, the security team, the government, and others. It fills up half of a 747. Not only that, the airline will have its security team. They also need time in advance to check out an already checked out airplane. Oh and I almost forget, there are the news media people, and the paparazzi will be waiting for you in New York."

"Do we have to go to New York," asked Ashley.

"Yes, the Queen can only authorize New York, and we have a list of permitted hotels, if you are going to use one," answered August.

"I saw the list of the hotels," said Ashley." I would like the New York Hilton. The Plaza is quite good, but I prefer the Hilton because of its location and excellent staff. The date is well in advance from now, and it is on my list of attendees."

"Okay, Duchess of Bordeaux," said August with a smile. "What would you like to eat?" "A cheeseburger, fries, and a chocolate milkshake," answered Ashley. "Just kidding."

TWENTY NINE

THE HOTEL

The New York Hilton hotel sits at the corner of 52nd Street and Avenue of the Americas, called 6th Avenue by the people, in Manhattan, a borough of the City of New York. It is a beautiful hotel in close proximity to Rockefeller Center, Central Park, and Radio City Music Hall, home of the famous Rockettes. There are more luxurious hotels in New York City, but the New York Hilton is in one of the best locations. It took less than a half hour to set it up through the event planner at the Bon Chic. In another half hour, all of the attendees were notified. August was a distinct whiz at managing events. His last item was a short note to the General giving Ashley's plans for the baby shower. The note was sent via a diplomatic dispatch addressed to Richard Hargrove, as requested.

The General responded by setting up a tentative meeting at the Hilton Hotel in a reserved presidential suite. The surrogate mother would be transported in an indistinguishable Mercedes sedan from Pebble Creek, New Jersey to New York

City, and enter the hotel via a special entrance used only by dignitaries. The date and time were also included in a return diplomatic dispatch so that August could manage the meeting with dispatch. The General would also be present but not engage in the meeting between Ashley and Emma. August confirmed the meeting, and scene was set for an American baby shower in the Hilton Hotel in the famous New York City.

THIRTY

THE BABY SHOWER

The announcement of a baby shower for the Duchess of Bordeaux in New York City was received with mixed emotions by the media. Some of the headlines in States and in London were almost humorous. August made a brief list of them for the Duchess.

"It is quite a list," said Ashley. "I personally asked the Queen for permission and she said permission is not required. Moreover, she said that being Royal is not a penalty, you may go as you please. She also said what you said that there would be a large British entourage to accompany me."

"Well, now we know," said August. "I'm really looking forward to it. It will be really nice not to be careful about what you say and do."

"I'm sure you don't know this, August," said Ashley, "that my family was very strict. I was brought up by my grandmother, who took her job very seriously. I can still hear her in my mind, commands such as 'walk right', 'watch what you say', 'you can't wear that outfit', 'eat carefully', 'don't talk with your mouth full', 'always put make up on before you go out', 'never smoke or drink in public', and lastly 'never ever have your picture taken with a glass in your hand'. Actually, I don't smoke or drink in the first place. So it will be great fun, even if my fun days appear to be over."

"It will be great for you Ashley. Can I still call you Ashley?" asked August.

"Of course," replied Ashley. "Don't be silly August. It will be pleasant to be called Ashley again. A person could forget his or her name around here. Oh, I almost forgot something. The royalty is not allowed to accept gifts from British citizens, but the queen did say that she didn't know if it applies to Americans. She just looked at me with a twinkle in her eye and said, 'why not try it?' The thinking seems to be that we are privileged and have enough."

"She seems to like you," said August.

"She does," answered Ashley. "There seems to be a connection between us. Possibly something in our individual backgrounds that I haven't recognized or even thought about. She is the most admirable person I've ever met. I am very fortunate."

"What about the gifts from the baby shower?" asked August.

"I talked to Michael, and I would prefer to open them here in his presence." replied Ashley.

"Sounds okay with me," said August. "Remember that when you are in the States, you are scheduled to meet with the surrogate mother."

The flight of the entourage to New York was without incident, and the U.S. Customs Service crew was as accommodating as possible. A limousine took the people of interest to the hotel, in flawless fashion. The operation was totally planned in advance and paid for by an anonymous donor. August thought he knew who the donor was, but he never said a word about that subject. The remainder of the British entourage rode to the Hilton in a luxury tour bus.

The baby shower in the New York Hilton was a total success. The guests were celebrities from TV, the stage, and screen, along with friends from Ashley's former life.

The shower lasted between two to three hours and Ashley was back in her room. August knocked and was admitted to the luxury suite.

August entered with a big smile, "You were wonderful, and I've heard that the guests really enjoyed themselves."

"It was very nice," replied Ashley. I'm both happy and sad. I enjoyed seeing my friends and former associates, and it was a distinct pleasure to chat and laugh with them. I really haven't laughed that much in many months. But, I have changed. I'm a different person now. Michael and I have a brand, and we're going to do great things and make a difference. At several points in the party, I asked myself, 'why am I doing all of this?'"

"I think you have changed Ashley; you **are** a different person," said August. "You are much more mature and have a goal – a big goal – for your life. Your other meeting will be in this suite at 6 pm today."

As planned, the armor plated Mercedes S Class arrived at the Hilton's celebrity entrance just prior to 6 pm. A lone woman was escorted to the luxury suite.

Emma Williams entered and was introduced to Ashley. The two ladies hit it off immediately, although there was no record of the conversation. The scheduled thirty-minute meeting lasted more than two hours. The position of nanny was discussed and both ladies agreed to it.

Emma asked Ashley if she would like to know the sex of the fetus, and Ashley said that she would.

"You will have a boy," said Emma. "It's for sure."

Emma and Ashley returned to their homes, and the baby shower in New York quickly became another memory. No photos of the shower and the meeting between the two ladies were ever taken.

THIRTY ONE

THE ROYAL BABY

As expected, Michael and Ashley were exceedingly private concerning their plans for the royal birth. Rumors were rampant. The royal couple were given a private residence, known as Malbec, off of the grounds of the palace, but on royal property. The royal couple had hired no staff persons. Baby-to-be was known as Baby Bordeaux.

Then on a fine crisp morning in February, the following sign with a blue border appeared at the Palace entrance:

> *The Royal Highness the Queen announces that the Duke and Duchess of Bordeaux have given birth to the newest member of the royal family. A baby boy was born yesterday at 6:30 am. The baby weighed seven pounds and three ounces.*

A few days later, the Queen announced that the name would be Philip George William Charles. Media attention to Michael and Ashley subsided.

The Queen was the first to view the newest addition to the royal family. The new parents appeared to be extremely happy, and Prince Michael publicly stated that he was proud to be a dad.

The royal news service issued a brief piece on the American nanny. Her name is Emma Williams, a nurse, a college educated person from the U.S. State of New Jersey. Her expected salary is in the range of seventy thousand pounds, equivalent to $90,000. The long journey had ended. No additional staff had been hired.

THIRTY TWO

THE FINALE

Emma Williams was exceedingly happy. She loved her position as nanny for the Duke and Duchess. The royal couple was perfectly matched, and there was very little discord of even the smallest nature between the two. The baby was a joy, and Emma was saving tons of money, since almost everything she needed was provided by the complicated royal system. The Queen often snuck out of the palace to visit the Baby Philip, and the relationship between them was a joy to behold. Emma thought there couldn't be anyone in the Universe who was as kind and pleasant as the Queen. Emma loved the Queen more than she loved herself.

Emma had Saturdays off, and she frequently went to the city center to view the people and visit the shops. She was never recognized as the royal nanny, and she liked that.

It was a beautiful Saturday approximately seven months after the baby was born. Emma had a delicious lunch in her favorite restaurant, and she then decided she wanted to buy something.

It would be nice to come home with a bag from a well-known store. After buying a pair of pretty shoes with 5-inch heels, that she really didn't need, she went for a short walk. She enjoyed the happy people as they went about their weekend chores. She often wondered what a person did for a living, and asked herself if they were as happy as she was. She ordinarily would have returned to Malbec, but life was good and she enjoyed just being outside and totally free to do whatever she wanted. She came upon Charing Cross Road and decided to cross it. She looked left and started off.

Then, like a flash, she was pulled from behind by a tall man. He fell backwards and she fell on top of him. The surrounding crowd was aghast. Then, they started clapping and were saying, "You saved her life. You saved her life." They both got up and the tall man was the first to speak.

"Are you okay Miss?" He was an American. Emma was shaken, but managed to say, "I am fine Sir. I do not know what happened." Then a passerby, said "We drive on the left side of the road Madam. You were almost hit by that taxi."

The tall man's wife said, "I have your package, Miss."

They went into an English pub on the corner, and all the people were clapping. The man was a hero.

One of the patrons asked, "Who are you Sir?" Then came the surprise of the day.

"My name is Robert Gildersleeve, I am an American movie producer, and I am here to find real-life characters for a movie I am producing on the royal baby. I think I have found the actors I came here to look for."

And do you know, Ashley, Michael, and Emma were in the movie, along with Matt and the General, as well as the baby boy Philip George William Charles.

ABOUT THE BOOK

This story is a total work of fiction. Nothing contained in the book is true and the persons involved do not reflect actual people. Names and places, except for minor exceptions, do not reflect actual entities. The New York City Hilton is the exception. It is a fine hotel located in midtown Manhattan that provides service worthy of royalty. The characters Ashley Wilson, Matthew Miller, General Leslie Miller, August Getraub, Pamela Givens, Professor Purgoine, and others do not exist in the manner reflected in the narrative. Coincidentally, persons with those names may exist somewhere in the world, but the author is not aware of them.

The story was not made into a movie in real life, and was included to end the tale on a cheerful note.

ABOUT THE AUTHOR

Harry Katzan, Jr. is a professor who has written several books and many papers on computers and service, in addition to some novels. He has been an advisor to the executive board of a major bank and a general consultant on various disciplines. He and his wife have lived in Switzerland where he was a banking consultant and a visiting professor. He is an avid runner and has completed 94 marathons including Boston 13 times and New York 14 times. He holds bachelors, masters, and doctorate degrees.

SOME NOVELS BY HARRY KATZAN, JR.

The Mysterious Case of the Royal Baby
The Curious Case of the Royal Marriage
A Case of Espionage
Shelter in Place
Life is Good
A Tale of Discovery
The Terrorist Plot
The Last Adventure
Lessons in Artificial Intelligence
On the Trail of Artificial Intelligence

Printed in the United States
by Baker & Taylor Publisher Services

Printed in the United States
by Baker & Taylor Publisher Services